THE CENTENNIAL LIBRARY COLLECTION

GIRL GUIDES OF CANADA

EDMONTON AREA

1967

The GHOST *of*

Follonsbee's Folly

The GHOST of
Follonsbee's Folly

Florence Hightower
Illustrated by Ati Forberg

HOUGHTON MIFFLIN COMPANY BOSTON

The Riverside Press Cambridge

FIFTH PRINTING   R

COPYRIGHT © 1958 BY FLORENCE C. HIGHTOWER
ALL RIGHTS RESERVED INCLUDING THE RIGHT TO REPRODUCE THIS BOOK
OR PARTS THEREOF IN ANY FORM
LIBRARY OF CONGRESS CATALOG CARD NUMBER: 57-12091
The Riverside Press
CAMBRIDGE • MASSACHUSETTS
PRINTED IN THE U.S.A.

For ROBERT

THE WAY Mr. Stackpole drove the family sedan you would think he had just robbed a bank and was making a getaway with a posse of state troopers in hot pursuit. Actually he was being pursued by nothing but his own impatience. He had just bought a house in the country, and he could not wait to get his family out to see it.

"You'll all love it," he cried. "I was terribly lucky to get it for so little. The real estate man had no idea of its value." He rounded a corner on two wheels. "That is," he went on, "from an architectural and historical point of view." He passed three cars in a spurt and swerved back to his own side of the road. "It's unique." He waved one hand, then hunched in a businesslike manner over the wheel and pressed harder on the gas.

From the seat beside him Mrs. Stackpole listened attentively. Placid by nature and accustomed to admire all that her husband did, she steadied the baby in her lap and swayed with the motion as relaxed and unafraid as if she were in a rocking chair.

1

"I've always wanted to live in the country." She smiled. "I think you are wonderful to find a house that's really big enough for all of us *and* the piano."

Absently, and in the nick of time, she caught the plump hand of Richard, the baby, as it was about to close on the tail of a gray cat who crouched, not at all relaxed, in the middle of the seat. Richard, who was six months old, grunted and continued to strain hopefully toward the cat.

"Tell us what it looks like," Mrs. Stackpole urged her husband.

"It's hard to do it justice." Mr. Stackpole's eyes gleamed. "It's a magnificent specimen of early American Gothic. It has a strange, fantastic beauty unlike anything I've ever seen, and the rooms are light and spacious." He was on the highway now, and he pushed the car to its limit.

"Is the living room really big enough for the piano?" Mrs. Stackpole leaned toward him, and with a crow of triumph Richard got the cat.

"Mother, look out!" Elsie Stackpole pushed forward from the back seat.

The cat struck with precision, and Richard's crow exploded in howls.

Mrs. Stackpole pulled Richard out of danger. "There, there." She patted him and rocked him on her knee. "Naughty Paddy!" She shook her head at the cat. "Go on about the living room."

"It's eighteen by twenty-five, not counting the

alcove." Mr. Stackpole swung the car into a curve. "Mark my words, Laura, your piano will sound better in this room than — "

"Please, Mother, please give me Paddy before Richard hurts her," cried Elsie, and as the car swerved she lost her balance.

A low, melancholy rumbling rose from the floor beneath Elsie's feet, and Tom Stackpole shouted, "Look out yourself, Elsie, you just kicked Buddy in the head."

Elsie recovered her balance. "What if I did? He's too dumb to know if he's kicked or not." She tossed her pigtails at Tom. Elsie was twelve years old, and she took no criticism from a brother a year younger.

"He is not dumb." Tom squirmed to get at his sister. He was separated from her, however, by an insurmountable obstacle. In the middle of the back seat, with Richard's twin brother Paul firmly clamped between her knees, sat Mrs. Angela Gittens, the Stackpoles' Negro cook. Mrs. Gittens' broad shoulders towered well above the heads of Tom and Elsie. The feather on her hat was bent double against the roof of the car and her knees, raised by the bulk of Buddy under her feet, rose like mountains to the nose level of the two children. She rolled her eyes menacingly, first at Tom then Elsie.

"You two be quiet or your daddy, God forgive him, will kill us all."

Hitting a steady sixty-five, Mr. Stackpole continued to talk happily about the piano and the living room and narrowly missed an approaching car. Mrs. Stackpole, enthralled by his words, relaxed her hold on Richard. Still tearful but persistent, Richard squirmed toward Paddy Paws. Paddy Paws, so named because she possessed seven toes on each foot, dug into the upholstery with both hind paws and one front. Her fourth paw she held ready, all seven claws bared.

"Mrs. Stackpole, you give me that baby." Angela extended two massive arms over the back of the front seat. Mrs. Stackpole responded instantly to the authority of Angela's voice. She handed back Richard.

"If you don't mind, Angela," she said, "though I'm afraid you're awfully crowded back there."

"We'll manage," replied Angela, and enlarging the valley between her knees she deposited Richard beside his twin.

"I'm squashed, Angela," Tom complained. "I don't see why I have to be squashed because Elsie wants to show the new house to her old cat."

"Paddy Paws has just as much right to see the house as your old — "

"That's enough," said Angela.

Tom sank back in his seat and stared out the car window.

"We're coming into the town now," announced Mr. Stackpole. He reduced his speed. "It's a pretty little town. Except for the Civil War monument, it's

4

just as it was when the house was built. Notice the churches, Angela. There are two of them and they're beauties." Mr. Stackpole half turned back in his seat. Angela's face grew rigid. She clamped the twins more firmly between her knees.

"The road, Mr. Stackpole. Watch the road."

Mr. Stackpole turned the wheel sharply. They missed the ditch.

"How good the country smells." Mrs. Stackpole breathed deeply. "I can't believe we're only twenty miles out of Boston."

"When was our house built, Daddy?" Elsie asked.

"About a hundred years ago. It's Gothic. Now Angela, there are the churches. Library's between them. Three stores, fine old houses, but wait till you see ours."

Elsie craned to see the library. Angela craned to see the churches, and Tom, squeezed in his corner, wondered how they could all get so excited about a bunch of buildings. Tom had been torn from a squirt gun fight to come on this expedition, and, furthermore, Angela had made him wash and change his shirt. He scowled at the fine old houses.

"Then," announced Elsie, "our house was built in 1850. That's before the Civil War."

"That's right, Elsie." Mr. Stackpole smiled and nodded. "I don't know the exact date. We must look it up. I think we'll find it's a house with an interesting history. It was in one family for a long time. Recently it's been empty. We turn off here."

In the back seat Angela braced for the turn.

"As soon as we move in I'll go to the library and find out about it." Elsie flicked her pigtails.

"Show-off," muttered Tom very softly so Angela wouldn't hear.

"A river!" exclaimed Mrs. Stackpole as the car rumbled over a bridge.

"River, fields, woods." Mr. Stackpole waved one arm and then the other. The car zigzagged. Angela's knees clenched the twins. Her lips moved soundlessly.

"Paddy Paws," exclaimed Elsie, "you can go mousing."

"Here's the drive." Mr. Stackpole turned off the road. The car bumped down a rutted lane. "A load of gravel will fix it," said Mr. Stackpole.

"An avenue of elms, how lovely!" Mrs. Stackpole ignored the bumps and looked up at the great leafless trees.

"That's the old stable," Mr. Stackpole gestured, "and here," he exclaimed, "is the house."

The rutted lane swung into a loop. Mr. Stackpole stopped the car and jumped out. As he started around to open the other doors and help Angela with the twins his eyes swept lovingly over the house, and for just a moment a shadow crossed his face.

"Now Angela," he said, "bear in mind that a coat of paint and a few minor repairs will make a big difference."

Tom was the last one out of the car, and then he devoted several minutes to persuading Buddy to follow him. Buddy finally emerged as a very large and hairy dog, a connection of the St. Bernard family. Buddy blinked, yawned, sighed, and shambling up to Tom, leaned his massive shoulder against Tom's hip. Buddy tried at all times to please Tom, but with a minimum of exertion to himself. When, as now, Tom's demands made sitting or lying impossible, he leaned.

The Stackpole family, with Angela towering in their midst like a major peak among foothills, gazed mutely at the new house.

The tall main gable confronted them with two wings flung out from it at right angles like the arms of a cross. Weatherbeaten gray paint, blistered and peeling, clung in shreds to the clapboards. The casement windows, framed in pointed arches and set with countless tiny diamond panes, peered out from the gray desolation in mild reproach, like eyes still fine, though sad and dim with age. The roof, rising at an alarming pitch, accentuated the height of the building, and from the edges of the roof hung an intricately carved wooden trim. Once white, now stained and broken, it drooped from the eaves, fragile, elegant and forlorn as a ruching of old lace. So unlike solid, ordinary houses and so like a faded apparition from another age was this lofty, lonely old mansion that Elsie, after giving it a sharp glance, caught her breath and stepped back as if she thought it might crumble and vanish before her eyes. Her pigtails began to quiver, a sure sign that she was worked up.

Mrs. Stackpole had stepped from the car with wide eyes and lips parted in a smile. She blinked at the house, rubbed her eyes, looked again hopefully, and, as nothing changed, two wrinkles appeared in her placid brow. Angela, after one long look, squared her shoulders, stuck out her chin, and clamped the twins more firmly to her bosom. Thus braced and ready, she glared at the house, challenging it to crumble if it dared. Tom, leaning into Buddy, looked

8

simply and sincerely blank. To tell the truth, all houses were alike to him. Mr. Stackpole, after scanning the intent but far from rapturous expressions of the others, appealed to Tom.

"Isn't it magnificent, Tom? Don't you want to move right in and fix it up the way it ought to be?"

Startled, Tom shifted his weight. Buddy, caught unawares, almost knocked him down.

"The carving on that vergeboard is the finest I've

9

ever seen, and the whole design has boldness and imagination. No sordid utilitarianism, no pinchpenny economies here. You see what I mean, don't you?" Mr. Stackpole went on eagerly.

Tom didn't see, but he wished with all his heart that he could please his father. His face screwed into a worried parody of his mother's.

"Yuh," he muttered and stared miserably at the house.

Mr. Stackpole turned to his wife. "Well, Laura, haven't you anything to say?"

Mrs. Stackpole started. "Oh yes, dear, yes. It's lovely, and when the shrubs come out and cover it up a little, it may be better."

"Laura," Mr. Stackpole pressed his hand to his forehead, "can't you see beyond the old paint and the minor disrepair? Can't you imagine it as it was in its prime and as it will be again? Can't you?"

"I'm trying," replied Mrs. Stackpole humbly, "but so far I haven't been able to."

Mr. Stackpole hung his head. Elsie's pigtails had been quivering more and more violently.

"Daddy," she shouted. "I know what you mean. It's like a beautiful, old-fashioned lady who's been waiting years and years for her lover who went away and never came back." Elsie shook all over as she strained for words. "It's faded and sad, but it's still beautiful. It's like a ghost." Her black eyes snapped. "It's haunted. I'm sure it's haunted."

10

A smile broke over Mr. Stackpole's face. He strode to Elsie and threw an arm around her shoulder.

"You've caught it," he cried. "Oh Elsie, what would I do without you?"

Elsie giggled, and Tom wished, not for the first time in his life, that he was bright like Elsie. The old house did look haunted, but he would never have thought to say so.

"Oh Daddy, there must be a ghost living in it. Don't you think so?"

"I'm sure of it," replied Mr. Stackpole genially.

Angela cleared her throat, and Mr. Stackpole turned to her. "That child's jumpy enough," declared Angela, "without ghosts."

"I like ghosts," said Elsie. "At least I think I do."

"We were just fooling," Mr. Stackpole apologized.

Elsie turned on her father. "I wasn't."

"There." Angela bobbed her head at Mr. Stackpole. To Elsie she said, "You forget about ghosts."

Mr. Stackpole bowed meekly. "Well, Angela," he asked after a moment, "what do you think of it?"

Angela eyed him solemnly. "I know you're a fine architect, Mr. Stackpole. I've listened to the things you've said about how houses should be built, and I've agreed with you, but this house doesn't fit." She cast a suspicious glance at the towering roof. "Are you sure it isn't going to fall down?"

Mr. Stackpole laughed. "It's solid as a rock."

"I'll take your word for it," replied Angela, "but

11

it doesn't look solid."

"We weren't expecting it to be so — so — " Mrs. Stackpole gazed helplessly at the peeling paint.

"Silly," said Angela.

"Silly?" Mr. Stackpole stiffened. "I'm disappointed in you, Angela. I thought you had better taste. Quaint and fanciful, yes; possibly a little overdecorated, but not silly." He stared defiantly at Angela.

Angela returned his stare. "To me it looks silly, especially the crochet work around the roof. What's it for? And those little diamond panes; why put in little diamond panes when big square ones let in more light?"

Mr. Stackpole scratched his head. "You are very reasonable, Angela, and practical. You'd make a better architect than I am."

"No, Mr. Stackpole, I wouldn't."

"I grant you," Mr. Stackpole went on, "that all houses look silly if they no longer serve a useful purpose. When this house has been cleaned up, and we are all living in it, with plenty of room for the twins and the piano and Aunt Elsie's furniture, with room for Buddy and Paddy Paws, which means anywhere from four to six kittens a year, with land for Tom and Elsie to play in, and a garden if you want it, then perhaps it won't seem silly. Then, perhaps, you will pause sometimes in your work to admire the delicate tracery of what you now call crochet work. Perhaps you will take pleasure in watching the play of sunlight

12

on the diamonds. Perhaps," Mr. Stackpole flung out both arms, his voice throbbed, "you will even come to feel a tender regard for Elsie's poor ghost."

While Angela listened to this speech her eyes opened wider and wider, and the twins slid slowly down her sides.

"Mr. Stackpole," she declared, "you should be a preacher. You can persuade a body into believing things that go against reason and common sense."

Mr. Stackpole bent his head to hide a triumphant little smile.

"You flatter me, Angela."

Angela hiked up the twins and marched toward the front door. "Let's go inside," she said.

WITH A FLOURISH Mr. Stackpole drew an enormous brass key from his pocket. While the others waited, he tried with all his strength to turn the key in the lock.

"Opened all right for the real estate man," he muttered, and sank to his knees for better leverage. "Just needs oil," he explained.

A hollow clank sounded, and with a groan the door swung slowly open. Elsie squealed.

"Warped," declared Angela.

Paddy Paws streaked between their legs and disappeared inside.

"Rats," said Angela.

Gingerly, for the floor boards creaked under their weight, they entered a high square hall. The white paneled walls and the ceiling were stained yellow and festooned with cobwebs. Just opposite the front door a staircase swept up in a graceful curve to the second floor. Mr. Stackpole shepherded the party through a door to the right and into the parlor, an enormous room with an alcove projecting toward the back of the house.

"There, Laura," he exclaimed, "isn't that perfect for your piano?"

Mrs. Stackpole's troubled face brightened. "Yes," she cried. "It's made for the piano and for Aunt Elsie's furniture too."

Angela halted just inside the door and held the twins tight while she tested boards in the floor. She stared pointedly at a stain on the ceiling and said nothing.

Standing tense in the middle of the room, Elsie darted sharp glances into the corners. On tiptoe, she approached and began to open each of a series of cupboards set in the wall. Tom listened to his parents' enthusiastic exclamations about acoustics and proportion. How, he wondered, could they find so much to say about a big, empty room? When Elsie had finished off the cupboards, she started ahead to explore the other rooms. Hoping that she'd scare herself into some kind of fit over a ghost or at least a rat, Tom followed.

With Buddy panting in the rear, they toured the library, the kitchen, the dining room and came back to the hall. Elsie stuck her nose into every cupboard and closet on the way. In the hall she discovered the door to a coat closet set inconspicuously in the paneling under the stairs. With an excited little squeal she

15

pushed open the door, stepped halfway in and backed out in haste sneezing and wiping cobwebs from her face. Tom giggled. Elsie tossed her pigtails, swept past him as if he weren't there, and started upstairs. Tom knew he'd nettled her, and, hopeful of more sport, went after her. Sighing at each step, Buddy followed. The circuit of the second floor was uneventful, but at the top of the staircase to the third floor Paddy Paws greeted them with a yowl.

"What is it, Paddy darling? What have you found?" Elsie pointedly addressed the cat as if they were quite alone.

Paddy rubbed against Elsie's legs, then darted off through a half-open door. Elsie ran after her. A sharp cry propelled Tom up the last steps. With a gleam in his eye, he too shoved through the door. Elsie lay on her stomach on the floor, but she wasn't having a fit. She was peering through one of the diamond-paned windows of an enormous doll's house. Tom stopped in his tracks. Never in his life had he seen anything like that doll's house, and yet, he had seen something like it. Had he dreamed about it? Was it — he trembled in spite of himself — some ghostly trick? He tiptoed closer.

Elsie rose to her knees. "Oh Paddy," she breathed. "It's just like the big house. Everything is just the same, even the trimming on the roof."

"That's it," Tom exclaimed in relief. "For a minute I thought I was seeing things."

16

He squatted beside Elsie, but she was now truly unaware of him. She opened two catches at the base of the doll's house and pulled up the front façade. It opened back on hinges until it rested against the roof. There, exactly as in the big house, were all the empty rooms, complete with paneling, fireplaces, cupboards, and closets. Paddy, who had evidently been waiting for this, slipped into the parlor. She was a tight fit, but she liked it so well that after a few preliminary turns she sprawled across the floor and began to purr. On hands and knees, Elsie poked her head into all the rooms she could reach, then she crawled to the back of the doll's house. The back lifted on hinges just as the front did. She emerged from the back rooms dusty and wide-eyed.

"Everything is the same," she exclaimed. "Everything."

She sat back on her heels, and as she continued to gaze at the house a smile spread over her face. "I'll fix it up," she announced. "I'll paint it and paper it inside just the way Mother and Daddy do the real house. I'll make it the most beautiful doll's house in the world." Pulling a handkerchief from her pocket, she spat on it and began rubbing at a diamond pane. Tom too had inspected the miniature rooms with growing fascination.

"Maybe I could do some painting on it too," he suggested.

Elsie remembered he was there. "No, Tom," she

said. "No thank you. I must do it myself. I know just how I want it. I'll make curtains and get old-fashioned furniture like Aunt Elsie's. I wonder where I can get old-fashioned furniture."

Elsie lapsed into deep thought, and Tom knew she had forgotten about him, about ghosts, about everything but the doll's house. He waited a minute, staring somewhat wistfully at the doll's house, then, reflecting that it was, after all, strictly a toy for girls, he stirred up Buddy and left Elsie to her thoughts.

A flight of winding back stairs deposited him and Buddy in the kitchen where Mr. and Mrs. Stackpole were discussing problems of modernization with Angela. Mr. and Mrs. Stackpole each held a restive twin, while Angela paced up and down, opening cupboards, pulling out drawers, and emanating an atmosphere of general disapproval. She lifted a lid from the old fashioned coal range and peered inside.

"All choked up with soot," she declared.

"I intend to get a new electric stove," said Mr. Stackpole.

"Expensive," muttered Angela. "Better to clean up the old one."

"We thought you might like a dishwashing machine too," put in Mrs. Stackpole.

"Unnecessary," returned Angela.

Tom's eyes wandered restlessly over the dingy old room and lighted on a contraption rather like the mouthpiece of a telephone set in the wall. He inspected it more closely. A little round brass door with a tiny hole in the middle covered the mouthpiece. Tom opened the door and squinted into a black tunnel. As soon as he took his hand off the door, it snapped shut.

"What's this?" he asked.

Mr. Stackpole laughed. "That's a very remarkable device." He strode to Tom's side. "It's a speaking tube."

"What's it for?"

"It's for talking to people on the third floor. Angela," Mr. Stackpole called, "come and see this. You'll find it a great convenience."

Angela eyed the mouthpiece suspiciously. "How?" she asked.

"This speaking tube connects with all the third-floor rooms. They were servants' rooms when the house was built. I think Tom and Elsie will like to sleep up there with you, Angela. By the way," Mr. Stackpole's eyes sparkled and he turned to Tom, "has Elsie found the doll's house yet? I expect she'll want the room it's in."

"She's found it," said Tom.

"Laura, wait till you see the doll's house. It's the most extraordinary thing."

"Excuse me, Mr. Stackpole," said Angela. "You were going to explain how I'd find this contraption a great convenience."

"Yes, of course." Mr. Stackpole turned back to

the mouthpiece. "When you want the children, Angela, you don't need to shout or climb three flights of stairs. You simply open the mouthpiece and blow. The air disturbance in the tube sets a diaphragm vibrating in each mouthpiece on the third floor. The vibration makes a whistling sound. Whoever is upstairs and hears the whistling goes to the nearest mouthpiece, pulls open the door and calls 'Hello.' Meanwhile the speaker at this end of the tube has put his ear to it." Mr. Stackpole tried to demonstrate, but with the twin bobbing in his arms it was impossible. "First you talk, then you listen," he explained. "Without raising your voice, you can carry on a conversation with the third floor. It beats the two-way radio hollow. There's no distortion, and, of course, it never gets out of order. Try it." He nodded encouragingly at Angela.

"Not right now. Not till we've settled about the sink. It's getting late." Angela spoke with gentle firmness as if she were dealing with an amiable but overexcited child.

Tom stood lost in thought before the speaking tube. Smiling faintly, he opened the door and blew into the hole. He cocked his head toward the stairs and listened. Nothing happened. He blew again. Still there was no response. Buddy ambled over and leaned against his thigh. Tom's smile stretched to a broad grin. He seized Buddy's collar.

"Up, Buddy, up."

Buddy tried to sink down on his belly.

"Up," Tom commanded.

With a groan, Buddy reared up and rested his front paws against the wall. Tom tugged his head close to the mouthpiece and held the door open.

"Speak, Buddy."

Buddy rolled his eyes at Tom in a bloodshot appeal designed to melt hearts of stone.

"Speak!" Tom pushed Buddy's nose as far as it would go into the tube.

Buddy tried to slide down to the floor. Tom propped him up. Buddy gave the agonized eye roll another try. Tom pushed harder on his nose. Buddy gave up, drew breath, and launched a deep and melancholy bay into the tube. The results were immediate. Elsie's scream came first. Next Paddy Paws ripped down the back stairs and disappeared under the stove. Seconds later, Elsie hurtled after her and flung herself at her mother. Abandoning Buddy, Tom slipped discreetly out the back door.

TOM FOUND HIMSELF in a clothesyard from which the ground fell in a grassy slope to the edge of a wood. He raced down the slope, crashed through brush and threw himself down behind a fallen log. At first his heart pounded so, he could hear nothing else. As his heart quieted down and he still heard no angry calls, he poked his head over the log. From the top of the slope the gray old house peered silently down through empty windows. No one appeared in the clothesyard. Tom got to his feet and wondered what to do next. Angela wasn't likely to let him get away with a trick like that. She might, to use her own words, be biding her time and storing up her wrath. On the other hand, she might, if left alone, forget the incident entirely. Tom continued to strain his ears for some sound, hopeful or otherwise. As no sound came, he slowly became aware that the silence to which he was listening was not silence at all. It was a blend of innumerable little rustlings, whisperings, and stirrings, with a soft, persistent swish underlying them all.

Tom was a city boy to whom all these woodland sounds were mysterious. He peered suspiciously into the underbrush. Suddenly a jay screamed, and he jumped as if he had been Elsie. The jay flashed out of a tree and swooped off, still screeching. Tom felt slightly silly. After the screech, the small noises — and especially the swish — took over more persistently than ever. Cautiously Tom pushed farther into the wood. As he proceeded, the sharp crunching of dry leaves and twigs beneath his feet changed to moist squunchings. Each time he paused the swish was louder. Suddenly, to his immense surprise, Tom found himself on the bank of a river.

In the chill blue light of the early spring afternoon the swiftly flowing water gleamed black and forbidding. Tom shivered. Then, as he watched the swirling current, he realized that he had tracked the swishing to its source. A glow of pride warmed him. He surveyed the river and the expanse of brown marsh on the far side. Feeling like an explorer he warily followed the bank upstream. A few small birds darted from the bushes and the jay screamed again. This time Tom didn't jump. He spotted the bird perched insolently on the top of a little round summerhouse. The summerhouse, popping up like a bandstand in the middle of the wilderness, spoiled Tom's feeling that his was the first human foot to tread this ground. He stared at it in annoyance until, realizing that it was all falling apart and grown over with bushes, he felt

24

reassured. Even if his wasn't the first foot, it was the first in a long time. Tom considered looking over the summerhouse but decided it was better to get the lay of the land first and come back to it later.

He went on upstream and in a few minutes came to a clearing. There, turned bottom up and wrapped in canvas, lay what could only be a rowboat. It knocked every other thought out of Tom's head. He ran to it, tried in vain to pull off the canvas, and threw himself on his stomach to peer up into it from underneath. In the darkness he made out the seats and a pair of oars stuck under them. Slowly he rose to his knees, while the possibilities of this discovery flashed in brilliant confusion through his head. He would follow the river with all its twists and turns. He could find the homes of the animals that lived in it and along its banks — frogs, snakes, turtles, beaver, muskrat, otter, moose, alligators, hippos. Tom was happily vague about the wild life of rural Massachusetts. He could fish from the boat. His heart jumped as he saw himself hauling great silvery flapping fish, one after the other, over the side.

Growing up in a city, Tom had learned to swim in a pool. During short summer vacations he had been taught to row and been taken on hikes. Never till now had he been able to imagine the carefree independence of the country boy who sets off, all unsupervised, to find his own adventures in woods and fields and along rivers. Still on his knees, Tom looked out in wonder at the river and the marsh. The sinking sun for the moment bathed both brown grass and black water in a golden summer light and washed away every trace of wintry grimness. Wide-eyed and absorbed as Elsie before the doll's house, Tom tracked moose, skinned beaver, and pulled in fish through an endless succession of summer days.

An approaching sound penetrated his daydream and brought him abruptly to his feet. This sound was neither new nor mysterious. It was the voice of Angela raised in a hymn. Tom listened attentively, for he knew by long experience that Angela's hymns indicated precisely as a thermometer the degree of her temper. The tune swelled and the words came clearly.

> By cool Siloam's shady rill
> How fair the lily grows!
> How sweet the breath, beneath the hill,
> Of Sharon's dewy rose!

Tom looked about him uneasily. This was a hymn he had never heard before, and, although both words and tune were pretty peaceful sounding, he couldn't be sure. If Angela had been singing the one about "His chariots of wrath the deep thunderclouds form, And dark is His path on the wings of the storm," Tom wouldn't have hesitated. He would have ducked quickly behind the boat and hoped that Angela wouldn't find him. After several moments of doubt,

Tom decided to take a chance on the hymn's being as peaceful as it seemed. He sat down on the boat and waited.

Angela loomed up at the edge of the clearing. Still singing she strode up to Tom, sat beside him, and finished the hymn in style. Her eyes swept over the river still golden in the sunset. She drew a deep breath and patted Tom's shoulder.

"I'm glad you're not mad at me," said Tom.

"I was mad when I started to look for you," Angela spoke mildly and continued to look at the river, "but as soon as I came out of the woods and saw the sunlight shining on the water, all my meanness began slipping away. I just stood there in the warm sun watching the water and feeling my aggravations slide off with it." She again patted Tom's shoulder, but her eyes rested dreamily on the river, and Tom knew she was speaking to herself more than to him. "That wreck your daddy's bought isn't even fit for a self-respecting ghost, but he's happy as a child with it and so's she, and with me to look after them, and the Lord's help, they'll come to no harm. Watching the river I knew it wasn't my place to judge others even though I'm nearly always right and they're mostly wrong. The ways of the Lord are inscrutable, and sometimes even I am wrong." Angela sighed, then tossed her head. "My troubles slipped away. I raised my voice in song. I felt as if I was young again and I was looking for Eddy to call him home. I came up here knowing I'd find you and we'd walk back together the way I used to walk with Eddy when he was a little boy." She turned gentle eyes on Tom. "I couldn't be mad at you now. I couldn't be mad at you any more than I could be mad at Eddy."

With Angela, moods of soft forgiveness were rare. Tom basked in her benign humor and felt especially fortunate in being compared to Eddy.

Eddy, Angela's only son, had died a hero in the Second World War. Angela seldom spoke of him. She was both too proud and too sad to mix his name with commonplace talk. Once in a while, when Tom and Elsie had pleased her especially, she had shown them the medal awarded to Eddy after his death and read aloud the citation which described his heroism. Eddy had volunteered to climb a steep Italian hillside in the dark of night in order to eliminate a German machine gun which was inflicting heavy injuries on the advancing Americans. When the Americans attacked again next morning, the machine gun had been silenced but Eddy had not returned to his platoon. During the seesaw fighting, which went on for days on that hillside, Eddy's dog tag was picked up among the rocks just below the abandoned machine gun. It was torn from its chain, probably by the same explosion that had demolished Eddy. The dog tag, the medal, the terse but thrilling words of the citation, and a few blurred snapshots of a big Negro boy in uniform were all that was left of Eddy, but for the

29

Stackpole children he stood above all other young men, black or white. Angela's opinion of all other young men was that they were lacking in character, otherwise they'd have volunteered and gone to Glory, or at the very least have got themselves a Purple Heart. Mr. Stackpole for whom Angela felt affection and some respect still did not come up to scratch, for he had got through the recent war with nothing more heroic than a bad case of measles.

"I'm glad you like it here, Angela," said Tom, "because I do too."

"Peaceful," replied Angela still looking out over the river.

"I'm going to explore the river," Tom went on. "I'm going to explore it in this boat we're sitting on, and I'm going to fish. The boat must go with the house."

Angela turned her attention to the boat. "You'll have a fine time on the river," she agreed. "A river's a fine place for a boy provided he can swim and that's one thing you can do, but," and Angela shook her head sagely, "any boat that goes along with that house will take a lot of repairs before it floats."

"I'll fix it," cried Tom. "I'll fix it so it's the best boat you ever saw, and I'll take you to row in it, Angela, if you want to."

"I'll be proud to go with you," replied Angela.

The sun had set. A chill wind rippled over the

water and set Angela's feather aquiver. The illusion of summer was gone. Angela stood up.

"Bless us," she cried. "Here I've been sitting and heaven only knows how your mother is managing with those twins. Come." She motioned Tom to his feet. "We can't stay now, but when we've moved here to live we'll come whenever we please. I'll sit in that old summerhouse and do the mending, and when you've fixed up your boat you'll take me rowing on the river as if I was the Queen of Sheba."

Gently she shoved Tom ahead, and bursting once more into the hymn about cool Siloam's shady rill she marched him back to the house.

From the top of the slope behind the house Mr. and Mrs. Stackpole were surveying their property.

"We have about five acres of land, Laura." Mr. Stackpole gestured proudly. "Right down to the river in back, as far as you can see downstream, and upstream not so much. The line is about at that stone wall in the middle of the field. The real estate man assured me there was no danger of the land's being built up. It all belongs to someone who has built a new house up there, just out of sight, and he wouldn't sell for anything. Wants the land for his own protection."

"It seems almost too good to be true," said Mrs. Stackpole.

GLENROSE SCHOOL HOSPITAL LIBRARY

4578

"Not a ranch house in sight!" exclaimed Mr. Stackpole. "Not a picture window or a two-car garage or a patio or a breezeway. You don't know what a relief it is to me to get away from patios and breezeways." Mr. Stackpole breathed deep. "Here there's just the fresh air and the old house and the fields and the river."

"There is one thing that troubles me," ventured Mrs. Stackpole.

Mr. Stackpole's face fell. "I think I know. It's Angela."

Mrs. Stackpole nodded. "I know she won't leave us, because she's adopted us and she's as devoted to us as we are to her, but I hate to have her so cross and disapproving."

"I'm what she disapproves of," said Mr. Stackpole. "She thinks I'm an extravagant and impractical dreamer and should be protected from my own incompetence. If she disapproved of the house for ordinary selfish reasons — because it was too far from church, or because there were too many stairs, or something like that — I wouldn't mind so much. It's her benevolent protective attitude that makes me uncomfortable."

"We can't get along without her." Mrs. Stackpole's forehead wrinkled. "We couldn't before we had the twins, and now with them we need her more than ever. She doesn't mind changing churches, and she's always said she'd like to live in the country and grow her own vegetables. I can't see why she should be so disapproving."

"She thinks I'm childish," said Mr. Stackpole. "Maybe I am, but that's still no reason for her to boss me around as if I were ten years old."

The strains of "By Cool Siloam's Shady Rill" burst from the wood at the foot of the slope. Mr. and Mrs. Stackpole listened closely. Mrs. Stackpole laid her hand on her husband's arm. A smile slowly erased all worry from her face.

"Richard," she whispered. "Angela's going to be all right. This isn't one of her usual hymns, but it's a contented one. I can tell by the tune even though I don't know it. She's decided to like it here. Everything is going to be all right."

Mr. Stackpole laughed, and in a burst of high spirits raced down the slope to meet Angela and Tom.

"Mother!" Elsie appeared around the side of the house. "I simply can't go on sitting in the car with those twins. I can't do it. They're perfectly awful, and I don't see why I'm always the one who's made to do these things."

"I'll be right there, dear." Mrs. Stackpole turned and ran in guilty haste toward the car.

CHAPTER 4

ACCORDING TO Mr. Stackpole's calculations, all necessary repairs to the house should be
finished by the middle of June and the family could
move in as soon as Elsie's and Tom's school let out.
However, as Angela took frequent occasion to point
out, "Man proposeth. God disposeth," and, in the
matter of repairs, Mr. Stackpole's calculations were
thwarted with an ingenuity, perseverance, and thor-
oughness that did suggest the intervention of a super-
human agency.

Rain fell daily during the month of May. The
roofers and painters were unable to work. When, in
June, the weather cleared and they got started, the
leaks in the roof had already finished off the plaster
on the third-floor ceilings. The ceilings fell out in
chunks and could not be replaced until the house
dried out. With rain falling in such abundance
from the skies, it struck Mr. Stackpole as odd that
there was so little water in the well, which (according to the real estate man) had provided a plentiful
supply for a hundred years. Mr. Stackpole called in

well experts. They disappeared inside the well and emerged an hour later, muddy and pessimistic. They could clean it out and patch it up, but they couldn't guarantee it through a dry summer. The best thing was to drive a new well and drive it deep. It ran into money, yes, but there was no telling when the town would get around to piping water out this far, and the way people used water these days, the well hadn't been dug that could keep up with it. Mr. Stackpole contracted for a driven well. The well was driven deep and the old well was covered with concrete, for Angela called up from the well of her memory and regaled the family with a wealth of stories about children (just the twins' age) who had fallen into wells and perished.

This should have settled the water problem, but it did not. There was still the pump. The pump, as described to Mr. Stackpole by the real estate man, was a superior piece of machinery, practically new. When the well experts heard this they laughed aloud. Sure they could patch it up so it would run, but they couldn't guarantee it would run steady. It seemed too bad, and they shook their heads, to spend so much on a first-class well and then not be able to get the water except with a bucket. Mr. Stackpole ordered a new pump, and this brought on the electricians. After an inspection, they reported that the wiring in the house had been installed by maniacs at the dawn of the electrical era. It was a plain miracle that the house hadn't burned to the ground fifty years ago. All the wiring must be torn out and replaced. Expensive, yes, but there was a law about house wiring, and they had to report to the building inspector. Mr. Stackpole knew about the law, but he wondered how the former owners had managed to evade it for so long. That was easy, said the electricians. The real estate man (his name was Creel) had owned the house for ten years. He had his own men install the pump and do the repairs. He rented the house out cheap until it got too run down for that and just stood empty. Mr. Stackpole had understood that Mr. Creel was the agent, that the owner was someone else. The electricians shook their heads and assured Mr. Stackpole that he wasn't the first one to be taken in by Mr. Creel.

Dashed and shaken, Mr. Stackpole reported this latest disaster to his family still in the city.

"I guess you're right about my being foolish and impractical, Angela," he said in conclusion.

Angela was passing a cherry pie. "Mr. Stackpole," she said, "it is better to be honest and foolish than wicked and full of guile," and she withdrew to the kitchen where, in lugubrious tones, she commenced the hymn:

> *Christian! dost thou see them*
> *On the holy ground,*
> *How the powers of darkness*
> *Rage thy steps around?*

3 6

July dragged by, hot and sultry, while the painters delayed the electricians and the electricians delayed the painters. Tom had bought fishing lines in May, but now he despaired of ever using them. Most of his friends were away for the summer. He hung around the house complaining that there was nothing to do. When Angela ordered him out from under foot he sallied forth to pick fights with other boys, throw baseballs through windows, tramp in flower beds, and pot at respectable citizens with the squirt gun. Complaints poured in, and finally the police paid a warning visit. Tom was yarded, and once more he hung around the house complaining that there was nothing to do.

Elsie retired daily to the basement of the public library where it was cool. There she drowned her disappointment in horror stories. She had nightmares regularly, and even in broad daylight sudden noises made her jump.

With everything packed and ready, Mrs. Stackpole could not even practice at the piano. The twins had heat rash. They whined a great deal, slept fitfully, and at the sound of the piano always woke and howled. Angela cooked and cleaned doggedly, but her hymns were all of the weepy "Oh Jesus, Thou Art Knocking" variety. Small annoyances infuriated her. Tripping over Buddy, catching Paddy on the kitchen table, Tom at the icebox, or Elsie looking under her bed at night set her off in a tantrum.

In mid-August the painters and paperhangers announced that they could not finish the downstairs because of other commitments which they had put off too long already. There just was more wall and ceiling than they had reckoned on. They would have to leave the parlor and hall until November when work slacked off. The hall alone, with all that old paint to be chipped off, would take a month, and as for the parlor they could do three complete decorating jobs in the time it would take to finish up a room that size. By this time Mr. Stackpole was so accustomed to disappointments that he accepted the painters' decision without a murmur. He and Mrs. Stackpole would finish the decorating themselves during his vacation and save some money. He engaged a company of professional housecleaners to clean up after the other workmen and to wash the windows.

The professional housecleaners drove out from the city, took one look at the diamond panes, and drove back. On the eve of moving day they presented Mr. Stackpole with a bill to cover their driving time and explained that they had a policy of never washing diamond panes.

"What now?" asked Mr. Stackpole.

"There's an evil spirit in the house," said Elsie. "We are doomed never to move in," and she shuddered.

Angela stalked from the kitchen. Her eyes were blazing. "Elsie Stackpole, if I hear any more of that kind of talk from you, I'll strap you until you can't sit down. Now Mr. Stackpole," she continued, "I can wash diamond panes, even if those professional," and she snorted, "housecleaners can't. You and Mrs. Stackpole do your parlor. Leave the twins and the cleaning to me. We are ready to move tomorrow. Let us not delay."

"Oh Angela," sighed Mrs. Stackpole, "it's more than we can ask you to do."

"The Lord will give me strength," replied Angela. She squared her great shoulders, her nostrils flared. "I'm going to pack the dishes now. The movers won't do it right."

She returned to the kitchen where, to the strains of "Onward, Christian Soldiers," she packed dishes until far into the night.

By the following evening the family was installed in the new house. Revived by carpentry and fresh paint, the poor faded beauty was her elegant, dressy self again. The crochet work gleamed crisply white. The green shutters hung straight, and even the dirty diamond panes managed to wink and glitter. Everyone went to bed early, and after the stuffy heat of the house in town the dim, high-ceilinged rooms were wonderfully cool and airy. For the first time in weeks the twins fell into deep, untroubled sleep. On the third floor Buddy stretched out under the open window of Tom's bedroom and snored. Paddy Paws went straight for the doll's house by Elsie's bed. She was expecting a new batch of kittens soon, and the doll's house was just the sort of establishment she had in mind. Except for Buddy's snores, the night slipped quietly by until a sort of screech followed by a thud broke the stillness.

Mr. Stackpole jumped from his bed and staggered downstairs where he went through all the rooms, turning on lights and searching for a marauder. Mrs. Stackpole groped her way to the twins' room and felt each bald head. The twins were sleeping soundly.

On the third floor everyone except Buddy sat up wide awake. Buddy missed a snore, sighed, and resumed his rest.

"Angela, Angela," called Elsie. "Angela, I'm scared."

Angela padded in and swept away Paddy, who was nervously pacing up and down Elsie's bed. "Now what's to be scared of?" Angela sat down beside Elsie and enveloped her with one enormous arm.

"That noise," quavered Elsie, and she burrowed close to Angela. "It sounded like — "

"Elsie Stackpole," Angela hugged her close. "You ought to be ashamed, a great girl like you, scared about nothing."

"But what was it, Angela?"

"I'll find out, and believe me it'll turn out to be nothing at all."

Angela went to the head of the stairs. "What was

40

it?" she called down to Mr. Stackpole who was returning from his search of the downstairs.

"It must be the pump," Mr. Stackpole called back.
"It needs adjusting. I'll fix it in the morning."

"There," said Angela, returning to Elsie. "It was
the pump."

"Don't go away, Angela."

Angela sighed and sat down again on Elsie's bed.
"Here you are twelve years old and the smartest girl
in your class," Angela hugged her again, "and you're
a bigger baby than when I first knew you."

"I'm not a baby," objected Elsie. "It's just that

I've read *The Hound of the Baskervilles* and you haven't."

Angela ignored this. "Do you remember the first day I saw you?"

Elsie snuggled close to Angela. "Daddy'd just come back from the war with the measles and he'd given them to Mother and I was keeping house."

"That's right." Angela chuckled. "You were only six years old, and you were keeping house just like a grown lady."

"Tom was no help," sighed Elsie.

"No, he wasn't," agreed Angela, "but you heated the soup and carried the trays upstairs, and you stood on a chair to wash the dishes. If you hadn't got the measles too you could have done all right by yourself. You weren't afraid of anything then."

"I was an unusual child," said Elsie. "No one else would come in to help because Tom and I and the measles were too much for them. Why did you come, Angela? You didn't know us then."

Angela sighed. "I was sad," she said. "It was just after I'd heard about Eddy. I wanted to work someplace where I was needed."

"You aren't sad any more, Angela? Not with all of us."

"No, I'm not sad, except when you don't do as you should."

"I should go to sleep."

"You should."

"Perhaps if you sang to me the way you did when I had the measles — "

Angela looked out the window at the stars. A breeze from the river rippled through the room bringing faint smells of damp grass. Very softly, so as not to waken the others, Angela sang "By Cool Siloam's Shady Rill."

"That's a new song," murmured Elsie, "but it's pretty."

"It's not new," said Angela. "I used to sing it to Eddy long ago."

"Sing it again."

Angela sang it again. Elsie nestled down under the covers, and before Angela had finished she was asleep. Angela tiptoed away. She looked in on Tom who, untroubled by ghosts, had gone back to sleep. Buddy snored regularly.

"A fine watchdog you are," muttered Angela. "Pump," she ejaculated under her breath. "Much he knows about pumps."

CHAPTER 5

NEXT MORNING the old house hummed
with activity. The twins howled for their breakfast.
Angela clattered in the kitchen. Mr. and Mrs. Stackpole dragged stepladders into the parlor and began
swabbing the ceiling. Elsie clambered up to the doll's
house, laden with buckets of leftover paint. Tom
whistled up Buddy and made off down the slope to
look at his boat.

During the summer the underbrush had grown
into a jungle of blackberry vines, alder shoots, and
clumps of choke-cherry. Tom tore his way through,
climbing, crawling, and getting thoroughly scratched.
Buddy discreetly let him break the trail until they
came out on the riverbank. Here the underbrush
gave place to lush grass and mud.

The river swished along, amber and gold-flecked
in the sunlight. Tom squatted on the bank to splash
water on his scratches. Buddy waded into the shallow water, took a drink, and with a grunt of contentment lay down in the water. He looked so happy,
with his eyes closed and the water lapping over his

shoulders, that Tom kicked off his sneakers, rolled up his pants, and waded in too. His feet sank delightfully into the muddy bottom, and cool, moist smells rose around him, tempering the midsummer heat. He waded out beyond Buddy until the cool flow of water became a definite tug on his legs and, fearful of losing his balance, he returned to the bank. Reluctantly Buddy followed him past the old summerhouse, so smothered now in blackberry and alder as to be almost invisible, and on to the edge of the clearing. Here Tom stopped dead in his tracks. In the middle of the clearing was the boat, turned right side up, and in the boat sat a young Negro man.

For a long minute Tom and the young man stared at each other in silence. Buddy lumbered up, leaned against Tom's hip, and blinked sleepily. The young man nodded.

"Hi," he said.

"Hi," replied Tom. There was another long silence.

"Nice morning," observed the young man.

"Yes," said Tom.

"Your dog?"

"Yes."

"Gentle?" The young man looked hard at Buddy who yawned and lazily waved his plume.

"Oh yes."

"Well, come in," said the young man. "Come right in, but just keep your hand on the dog."

Tom took a step forward, stopped, and gazed in puzzlement at the young man who had bent down inside the boat. When he straightened up again, he made a friendly gesture with the paintbrush he was holding.

"Anything I can do for you?" he asked politely.

Tom swallowed. "Why are you — " he began. "I mean did someone tell you to paint that boat?"

"No sir," replied the young man. "I'm doing it of my own free will." He swiped the brush along the bottom of the boat, then sat up to admire the result.

"Didn't Angela tell you to paint it?" Tom took another step forward and stopped.

"Nobody told me to paint it," returned the young man. "Why should they?" He grinned at Tom.

Tom's face screwed up in distress.

"What's the matter, son?" The young man put down his paintbrush. "You feel sick?" He peered anxiously at Tom. "Eaten too much?"

"No," Tom shook his head, "but you shouldn't be painting my boat if no one told you to."

"Your boat?" The young man's broad and genial face lengthened in pained astonishment.

"I found it," explained Tom, "and Angela said it went with the house."

The young man shook his head and rubbed one hand back and forth over his forehead. "It's my boat," he said slowly. "It was four years ago, but I remember. I found it laying here all beat up and half full of water, and I rebuilt it and painted it, and no one ever come by to claim it. If it was your boat, why didn't you speak up?"

Tom's brain rocked. "I couldn't. I just moved here last night, but Angela said the boat went with the house, and, gee, I've been waiting for ages — "

"Hold on." The young man pressed his hand against his forehead. "Look," he said, "let's sit down and figure this out." He put down his paintbrush, climbed out of the boat, and sat down on the grass. "You claim this boat goes with the house?" he asked after a long and thoughtful pause.

"Yes, and Angela thought it did too, and she's always right."

"Angela?" The young man rubbed at his forehead again. "Who's Angela?"

"She's our cook," explained Tom, "and she tells everyone what to do."

"She don't tell me what to do," said the young man with spirit. "I'm independent." He jerked his head. "Let's leave her out," he suggested. "It's confused enough without dragging in a third party." He stared at the ground while he collected his thoughts. "Now, where were we?" He turned to Tom.

Tom shook his head. "I don't know. It's just that Angela said, and so I thought — "

"Sit down," the young man interrupted, "and be comfortable. You'll find it's easier. Just keep your hand on the dog, if you don't mind. We gotta figure this out right." Tom squatted down while the young man wrinkled his forehead and screwed up his eyes in a paroxysm of thought. "I've got it," he cried. "I claim it's my boat, but you think you got a claim to it too. You gotta state your claim. That's it, and then we'll go on from there. Now go right ahead." He nodded encouragingly at Tom.

Tom told how he had found the clearing and the boat, how excited he had been, and how he had waited and waited until, finally, just this morning, he had thought he was going to be able to launch it. The young man chewed a blade of grass while he listened with grave attention.

"So you just moved into that big old house on the hill," said the young man when Tom had finished.

"Just last night."

"That explains it." The young man frowned. "I just come myself yesterday, but not for the first time. I been coming here for years. You see," he went on, "I found that boat first four years ago when nobody was in that old house at all, and I rebuilt it. I think I got the first claim."

Tom sighed. "You found it first." He looked at the boat and sighed again. "I didn't think anyone else ever came here. I thought I'd sort of discovered the place and the boat too." He dug his heel into the ground.

Buddy, sensing his unhappiness, rose up from his

48

rest to lean against Tom's shoulder and lick his neck. The young man moved uneasily.

"I know how you feel," he said, "because I feel the same way about this place. I feel like it was mine, and nobody else knew about it. It is mine too. I was coming here before anyone else."

"Yes," muttered Tom.

"But," the young man went on soberly, "I don't want you should be disappointed, and maybe you have got some small claim to the boat because it might have gone with the house only I found it first." He stared at the ground deep in thought. "I tell you what." His face lighted. "You can come out in the boat with me whenever you want. How's that?"

"Gee," Tom grinned, "thanks."

"Don't mention it," replied the young man. "It's only justice." He sank back until his head rested on the grass. "That took some figuring," he sighed. "I'm all wore out."

"Can we go exploring and fishing?" Tom asked.

"You bet," said the young man. "Bass," he sucked his lips, "fried in butter." He smiled dreamily at the sky. His smile faded. "Gotta paint the boat first." He rose to his elbows. "I was so wore out with figuring I forgot."

"I can help you." Tom jumped up. "If Elsie can paint, I guess I can too."

"Elsie?" the young man asked. "I thought it was Angela."

49

"Elsie's my sister," explained Tom. "She's paint-ing a doll's house."

"Oh," the young man pursed his lips, "I guess you got a pretty big family living up in that house."

"Yes," said Tom, "that's why my father bought the house, because there are so many of us." He enumerated the members of his family while the young man selected a new piece of grass and chewed on it.

"And what's your name?" inquired the young man. "If you don't mind my asking."

"Tom."

"My own name's Joe." The young man extended a huge hand. "Pleased to meet you, Tom." He shook Tom's hand.

"Pleased to meet you," replied Tom and added shyly, "Joe."

"Now Tom." Joe chewed on the grass, "I'm real glad to know you and to take you out in my boat, but, no reflections on nobody, and no offense meant, I don't want to take out your whole family."

"You don't need to," Tom put in hastily. "They're all too busy, but," he added after a minute, "Angela did say she'd like to go out on the river."

The young man scowled. "That's the bossy one."

Tom blinked. "Yes," he said, "I guess she is."

The young man sat straight up and rubbed his forehead again. "This is hard to explain without offending, and I don't want to offend no one, but

I'd be obliged to you, Tom, if you just didn't say anything about me and my boat to the rest of your family. It's not that I got anything against them." Joe eyed Tom solemnly. "They got a right to live in that house, and if one of em's bossy, she can't help it, I guess. But this is my vacation. I work all winter, off and on, so's I can have a quiet vacation in this place of mine and lay around and fish. I don't mind you coming here. You seem quiet and nice, and you got some claim, but if all the others come too," he wrinkled his nose in distaste, "they'll spoil it. They'll scare the birds and fish, and, well, how can I swim and lay around in the sun with all them women looking on?" He held out both arms in appeal.

Tom understood, and deep in his stomach he felt a lift of excitement at having a secret from Elsie and Angela. "I won't say anything," he assured Joe. "I know how you feel."

"Shake on it." Joe grinned. Once more he extended his huge paw and wrung Tom's hand. "My mind's at rest," he said, and sank down again on his back.

"You don't mind Buddy?" Tom asked, suddenly anxious. "Buddy's my dog."

Joe rolled his head to examine Buddy who was fast asleep. "No, he seems real gentle. Not much of a watchdog I guess. I don't mind him." Joe shut his eyes. "If you want to paint on that boat, you're welcome to. I'm all wore out with brainwork."

Tom climbed into the boat. The paint was dazzling green. He laid it on in broad strokes. As the sun beat down and the river slid by and the shiny green area grew under his brush, he felt a glow of contentment and a thrill of expectation exceeding even that of the early spring day when he first found the boat. Without thinking he began to hum Angela's tune about cool Siloam's shady rill. As he swept the brush back and forth along the ribs of the boat, he hummed louder, again and again.

"That's a pretty tune," said Joe, still flat on his back. "Where'd you learn that?"

Tom blushed. He had thought Joe was asleep. "I heard it somewhere," he muttered.

"It's pretty," said Joe, "real pretty." He sat up and scratched the back of his neck. "I like songs," he said, "and that's another reason I like this place. There's songbirds in this woods." He reached down inside his shirt and went at his shoulder blades. "You know the songbirds?"

"No," replied Tom, "except maybe gulls or bluejays."

"They ain't songbirds," said Joe. "They just screech. But you lay here quiet for a while, and you can hear five or six songbirds singing their songs." Still scratching between his shoulder blades, Joe cocked his head. His broad good-natured face sharpened to attention. He kept on scratching, but absently.

"Oriole," he said. "Song sparrer." He stopped scratching altogether, and his face lighted. "There's the wood thrush. Hear him?" Joe lowered his voice to a whisper. "There he goes again. He's got an awful pretty song."

Tom stopped painting and cocked his head like Joe. The wood, now that he listened, was full of chirps and twitters.

"He's right nearby," Joe scanned the treetops, "but he's shy. He don't show himself."

Tom listened harder than ever to the confusion of little sounds. Smoothly, like a cat, Joe drew his legs under him and began to crawl on hands and knees across the clearing. He motioned Tom to follow, then put his finger to his lips and listened a minute before crawling on. Tom crawled after him into the underbrush, pausing when Joe paused, listening vainly for some pattern in the chorus of twitterings. Joe stopped, pointed into the leaves and motioned Tom to come up beside him. He pointed again. Tom peered into the treetops. Joe touched Tom's shoulder, and as Tom turned to him he whistled a soft trill of notes. From the leaves above came an answering trill, and Tom spotted a bird with a speckled breast perched just above them.

"There," cried Tom. "There he is," and the bird darted from sight.

Joe sighed. "That's no way to watch birds. You gotta keep quiet."

They returned to the clearing, and while Tom worked on the boat Joe lay on his back with his eyes closed. Every now and then he said, "Song sparrer," or "swamp sparrer," or "veerio," and Tom, looking up from his painting and straining his ears, scanned the trees in vain. The wood was all a-twitter with bird songs, but the singers were hidden in the leaves and Tom couldn't for the life of him separate one song from the general chorus. Suddenly, like a flame, a bird swooped low over the clearing, flashed upward, and lighted on the outermost tip of a branch. There it swayed and swung in full, flashing view, its head and wings jet-black, its breast brilliant orange. Tom opened his mouth to shout and remembered just in time not to. The bird swung on its twig like a trapeze artist, then gave a sharp whistle.

"Oriole," said Joe without opening his eyes.

The bird whistled again, hopped to another twig, and swung on it more daringly than ever. Joe pursed his lips and whistled. The oriole, swinging for all he was worth, answered Joe's whistle, and for several minutes they conversed until, with a sudden harsh cry, the oriole flew off among the trees.

Lost in wonder, Tom had forgotten his painting. "I wish I could whistle like that," he said.

"Maybe you can," replied Joe, "but you gotta practice."

"If I could just remember how the oriole whistled."

Joe rose on his elbow. "Listen," he said. "The song goes like this, mostly, only sometimes the tune's a little different." He whistled slowly and clearly.

Tom tried to imitate it, and Joe patiently repeated the same series of notes until he felt Tom was showing improvement.

"That's fine," he said. "Now you just keep at it and keep listenin' for the bird. I'm going to catch me some frogs for lunch."

He stretched, scratched, and rose to his feet. He extracted a fish net from a duffel bag lying near the boat. "If I get a good catch, I'll invite you to lunch. You like frogs' legs?"

Tom's eyes widened. "I never had them. Angela never cooks them."

"Well," said Joe a trifle stiffly, "Angela, for all she knows so much, is missing a rare treat," and he set off for the river.

Tom rather wanted to go too and see the frogs being caught, but Joe hadn't invited him, and since he was Joe's guest, he felt a certain hesitation about forcing his company. He resumed his painting and whistling. He had almost finished the inside of the boat when, with a thrill, he thought he recognized the oriole's whistle, faint and far away but quite distinct from the other twitters. Again he picked up the song, and again he whistled. His whistle, he felt, almost caught the carefree rhythm of the oriole's. Whistling and listening, he was laying the last strokes of paint on the seats when Joe returned from the river, holding his net out in front of him.

"Joe, I heard the oriole again, and listen to this." Tom whistled.

Joe's face crinkled into a grin. "Good boy. You just about got it. You're talented, that's what."

Tom flushed with pleasure, but Joe's grin faded as he said, "I meant what I said about inviting you to eat frogs' legs with me, but frogs are poor this season. There's scarce enough for one, I'm afraid, let alone two." He poked the net under Tom's nose. "You can see for yourself. It's a poor catch."

Tom looked at the palpitating mess of frogs in the bottom of the net. "It's all right," he said. "I don't mind."

"I hate to disappoint you like this." Joe shook his head sadly.

One frog lifted its head from the mess and fixed Tom with a gelatinous eye. Tom's stomach heaved.

"I don't mind. Honest I don't," he said.

"You're a real gentleman." Joe spoke with unconcealed admiration and sat down with the net between his knees. Drawing a hunting knife from his belt, he set about butchering the frogs. Tom watched for one horrid minute then turned away swallowing.

"I better be getting back home," he said.

"That's right," agreed Joe. "You must be hungry." He continued to work with the knife. "You come back after you've eaten, and we'll do the bottom of the boat."

"When will you be through — eating, I mean?" Tom asked unsteadily and with averted eyes.

"Won't take me long," replied Joe. "I just roll 'em in bread crumbs and fry 'em in butter over a hot fire."

"I'll be back," Tom promised, "when you've finished." He whistled up Buddy and made for home.

In the clothesyard near the back door Tom made a wide circuit of the twins, who hauled themselves to their feet, shook the sides of their play pens, and hailed him with howls. The kitchen was empty. From the living room came the murmured conversation of Mr. and Mrs. Stackpole hard at work. From upstairs came the buzz of the vacuum cleaner. Tom blew into the speaking tube. The buzz stopped, and a moment later Angela's voice came down the tube.

"Who's that?"

"It's me, Tom."

"Oh. Your lunch is in the icebox. Just sandwiches till I get through this cleaning. Everyone else has eaten. Pour yourself some milk and wipe up your crumbs and be back on time for dinner."

"O.K., Angela," said Tom and hung up.

He ate his sandwiches slowly. Angela made good sandwiches, and while he chewed, Tom kept his mind firmly fixed on their flavor. Thoughts of Joe, nice as he was, led to thoughts of frogs' legs, and thoughts of frogs' legs — Tom stuffed his mouth with ham sandwich and concentrated his whole attention on it.

As he passed through the clothesyard on his way back to the river the twins howled more frantically than before. Tom felt quite sorry for them, penned up that way with nothing but a few old rattles and things to play with. He paused a minute considering what he might do to relieve their suffering. Like crazed prisoners, the twins extended their fat arms through the bars of their cages, raised their swollen faces, and wailed most piteously. Tom backed away. If he got mixed up with the twins now, Angela might make him take care of them and he wouldn't get away for the rest of the afternoon. He suppressed his charitable instincts and hurried off down the slope.

IN THE CLEARING, by the embers of his campfire, Joe lay asleep. His frying pan, still coated with crumbs, was flung to one side in the long grass. Tom sat down near the frying pan to wait and to listen again for the oriole. In the afternoon heat, the bird songs seemed to blend with the other rustlings and hummings into a single drowsy mumble. Above this mumble Tom heard an ocasional harsh rattle or shrill whistle from the river, but not the song of the oriole. Perhaps, like Joe, he was taking a nap. Dapplings of sunlight slipped and quivered over Joe, over the boat and the grass. Moist smells of mud and moss combined with whiffs of wood smoke to scent the air with a warm and soothing fragrance. Tom leaned back and rested his head on Buddy. He closed his eyes and was floating on the edge of sleep when a rustling close to his side roused him. He opened his eyes to see a tiny brown bird perched on the edge of the frying pan only a few feet away. The bird teetered and jittered there with its little jerky tail pointing straight up behind. Quivering with excitement from the tip of its beak to its last tilted tail feather, the little bird hopped into the pan and went at the crumbs for all it was worth. Tom held his breath. While the bird devoured the crumbs, it darted efficient glances from side to side and flipped and dipped its tail with such a bustle of watchful efficiency that Tom, trying not to move a muscle, almost choked with laughter. Sometimes when a beady and self-confident little eye looked right at him, and the tail jerked up another notch to an even more improbable angle, Tom was tempted to shout "Boo," and give the conceited little thing a scare. The scare came suddenly and without help from him. The scream of a jay ripped through the afternoon. Chattering, the little bird flipped away and the jay himself bounced down beside the frying pan.

"Get out of here, you screeching old jay bird."

Tom turned to see Joe sitting straight up and shaking his fist after the retreating jay.

"Wakes me up and scares off the little birds that come to the fry pan," grunted Joe.

"It was a little tiny bird with a tail that stuck straight up," said Tom.

"A wren most likely." Joe lay down again.

Tom went on describing the little bird, while Joe smiled sleepily.

"It was a wren all right, and you was lucky to see it so close. You see, it's like I said, you just gotta lay still." Joe yawned, closed his eyes, and lay so still that Tom was afraid he'd gone to sleep again.

"How about the boat?" ventured Tom.

"You go right ahead and paint." Joe snuggled his shoulders into the grass.

"I can't turn it over alone."

"Well, there's no hurry. Just lay still — "

"But tomorrow we're going fishing and catch a bass."

Joe rose with a sigh. "You're right," he said and helped Tom turn the boat.

Very slowly, through the afternoon, they painted. They paused often while Joe picked out bird songs and whistled them back. They made a lengthy sortie in search of a rose-breasted grosbeak that Joe heard calling from the woods, and on the return trip they took time to refresh themselves at a patch of early-bearing blackberries. The sun was beating hot and slantwise into the clearing when Tom smoothed the last brush stroke onto the boat and squatted back on his heels.

"There," he said with satisfaction and then whistled the song of the oriole just for practice.

Reclining in the grass Joe grinned his approbation. "That's a fine piece of work we done," he said, "and," he added, "you done most of it." He rubbed his shoulder blades in the grass. "What do you think about a swim?"

"In the river?" Tom jumped to his feet. "Let's."

"Now take it easy." Joe sat up and looked Tom over. "How good a swimmer are you?"

"I'm pretty good," Tom assured him. "Even Angela thinks I'm a good swimmer."

Joe grunted. "I guess you gotta be good to please that one." He rose to his feet. "But just the same, I want you should be careful and do what I say. There's current in that river."

On the bank they took off their clothes, and Joe gave instructions.

"You see that big oak down there and the spit of land just beyond?" He pointed downstream and Tom nodded. "From here," Joe went on, "you dive right out into the current. It'll sweep you along so's you feel like a fish. All you gotta do is flip your tail and you just glide, but as soon as you get up to the oak tree, you break for shore and you'll come to slack water and hard bottom just this side of the spit. If you miss the spit, you keep going till you smack into the bridge if you're lucky, or go way on down and over the falls if you're not. You think you can swim good enough?"

"I think I can," said Tom.

Joe nodded. "I'm going first, and I'll be standing as far out by the end of the spit as I can to catch you if you miss, but it's better not to miss. Now watch me and remember about the oak tree."

Joe dived into the water, and a moment later his

head bobbed up in midstream. "Here I go," he called, and go he did.

Resting on his back, lifting his head to grin back at Tom, waving first an arm, then a leg to show how he wasn't swimming, he swished merrily along with the current. At the oak tree he flipped onto his stomach. His black arms flashed up and down with the power and faultless rhythm of a machine. A foaming wake surged up behind him. Very slowly at first, then with a spurt, Joe moved in toward the bank, while Tom waved his arms and cheered this marvelous exhibition of form and strength. It wasn't until Joe stood up in the shallow water, breathing hard and shaking the water from his ears, that Tom began to feel a slight uneasiness. He was glad, at any rate, that he'd only said he was a pretty good swimmer. It would have been awful if he'd boasted to Joe, who swam far better than the instructors at the pool. Even Joe had had to swim hard to get out of the current. Tom stared at the slippery water and a shiver ran through him, despite the hot sun. He remembered that tug on his legs when he had waded in the morning.

"Come on," called Joe. "I'm ready for you." He was standing up to his knees in the water at the end of the spit. "It's great," he shouted, "but remember the oak tree."

Tom drew in breath and made a long shallow dive. When he opened his eyes, the water below him was cloudy amber flecked with little black specks all sliding away downstream into darkness. Before he'd come up from his dive, he felt the cool slippery fingers tugging him along too. I'll turn back, he thought, but it was too late. As he came to the surface, the current snatched him, and he was off, helpless as a leaf or a bubble. For a minute, he felt a sickening fear, but as he whirled along more swiftly the fear was swept away and transformed into a wild and dreamlike excitement. He was swooping as effortlessly, as magnificently, as the oriole on the wing. He laughed, he waved his arms and legs, he buried his face in the amber water, sure, for the moment, that in this enchanted element he had no need for breath. He was a god, tireless, all powerful, swooping, gliding, flashing about in a cool amber heaven. A yell disturbed his dream. He lifted his head and saw Joe like a black tree up ahead wildly waving its branches. Tom remembered the oak tree, and there it was coming up. Serenely confident in his godlike strength, and to please Joe who was his friend, Tom struck out for the tree. It slipped away behind. He swam harder, pressing for the bank, but the bank raced along without coming closer. Tom set his jaw and swam as he had never swum before. Still the current swept him down, not with an exhilarating rush, but with a cruel, unrelenting insistence. Tom was having to breathe again, painfully. His legs ached. His arms, scooping back the water, were heavy as lead. He shut his eyes and forced those aching legs and leaden arms to beat and beat against the current, while each sharp drawn breath stabbed like a knife. Suddenly, and just in time, for the pain of breathing was unbearable, the current slackened. Tom's legs sagged down, and his feet touched pebbles. He opened his eyes to see the spit with Joe squatting on its bank and grinning.

"Great, ain't it?" cried Joe. "Better than ever this year, on account of the river's so high."

"Gee," was all Tom could say. Panting and shaking, he waded to Joe and collapsed beside him.

"It's better'n the roller coaster," said Joe. "I thought you could make it," he went on, "but I'd of caught you if you'd missed."

"For a minute," panted Tom, "I thought I was going all the way down."

"But before that," Joe's eyes shone, "when you just swoosh along, there's nothing like it. Nowhere."

"Boy," said Tom. He was getting his breath at last. "Boy, I'm glad I did it."

"Come on," Joe stood up, "we'll do it again."

They did it again and again until, cool and weary, they lay down with Buddy in the clearing to bask in the hot rays of the setting sun.

"You know," said Joe, "I'm real glad you found this place."

"So am I," said Tom.

"Just at first," continued Joe, "I weren't quite sure.

Nothing personal. It was just that this is my place, and, well, I like to keep it private. People kinder bother me, but you don't. You like the birds, and you can swim, and your dog's real quiet. I don't mind you here at all."

Tom stretched luxuriously. "I'd like to camp out with you all the time. I never had so much fun." His eyes wandered over the clearing and lighted on the frying pan. "I bet I'd like frog's legs if I tried them."

Joe sat up. "My," he said, "I'd better be thinking about supper." He pursed his lips and a gentle, far-away look came into his eyes.

"What are you going to have?" asked Tom.

"String beans?" murmured Joe, "Summer squash?" He smiled. "Summer squash stewed up in butter with a little onion. Mushrooms maybe." After a pause he added, "Tomatoes," and stood up with sudden energy.

Tom stood up too. "Are you going to get them now? Can I come with you?"

"No. No thank you." Joe started toward his duffel bag.

"I don't mind walking to the store," Tom went on eagerly. "I could help you carry — "

"No, no," Joe shook his head decisively, "thanks just the same, I'll manage." He rummaged in the duffel bag. "Won't they be expecting you home?"

"It's too early," replied Tom.

Joe rose up from the duffel bag. He rubbed his head and bit his lower lip. "Maybe it's not so early as you think. That Angela," he swallowed and rubbed his head harder than ever, "maybe she'd be mad if you didn't get home right about now. Maybe she'd make you stay in tomorrow and work or something, and, well," Joe looked at Tom, then quickly dropped his eyes, "maybe she would, and you couldn't go fishing like we planned."

Tom saw the sense of this. "I guess you're right," he said.

Joe grinned and nodded encouragingly. "You get along home now and be back tomorrow after breakfast. We'll catch us a bass."

"O.K." Tom started away.

A minute later he remembered Buddy and turned to whistle for him. Joe was standing by the duffel bag staring thoughtfully at two burlap sacks, one large, one small, which he had laid out on the ground. He didn't notice when Buddy rose with a grunt and lumbered after Tom.

In the clothesyard Tom again encountered the twins. They were sprawled across the floors of their play pens and seemed to be sleeping until, as Tom drew near, first Richard (Tom could tell him because of the way his ears stuck out) raised a flushed and smeary face and moaned. Paul, flat on his back, broke into a whimper. Tom felt sorry for them. He lifted first one then the other from the pens. If Angela didn't mind, he'd play with them until it was time for their bath and supper. They looked as if they needed cheering up, and as he lugged them toward the house they clung to him in a manner that was most flattering.

THE KITCHEN, as Tom entered, resounded to the music of the piano. Chicken was
frying on the stove, and Angela was rhythmically
rolling out pie crust at the kitchen table.

"Angela," Tom announced, "I'm right on time,
and I've brought in the twins — "

Angela's rolling pin thudded to the floor. "Oh
Lord," she cried, "strike me down." She snatched
the twins from Tom and sank with them into a chair.
"My suffering babes," she moaned and rocked back
and forth, "my poor innocents!" Her face contorted,
her voice rose in anguish, and the twins now broke
into wails which mingled dismally with the lament
of Angela and the notes of the piano.

"What is it, Angela? What have I done?" cried
Tom.

"You," cried Angela, "you have done nothing.
You are as innocent as the precious lambs themselves." She pressed the lambs to her bosom until
they wheezed for breath. "It is I, I who have sinned.
Oh Lord, send a whirlwind, send a pestilence." She

tilted her head toward the ceiling. "I await the coming of Your wrath. Hold it not back."

"Angela," shouted Tom, "what's the matter?"

Angela fixed him with a tragic glare. "I forgot them. They've been out there since morning. The vacuum cleaner drowned their cries. Oh Lord, strike me down!" She swayed in anguish, and the twins howled wearily on.

"But they're all right," Tom tried to comfort her. "They're just hungry. I'll get Mother."

"No," shouted Angela, tightening her grip on the twins, "I promised to look after them. I gave my word." She rose and started for the kitchen stairs.

"The chicken's burning," said Tom. "Hadn't I better call Mother?"

Angela turned. Her eye fell first on the smoking chicken and then on the pie crust. With an effort, she pulled herself together.

"Your mother has been washing the ceiling all day. She's worn out." Suddenly she thrust the twins at Tom. "You and Elsie," she said, "you can bathe them while I fix their supper." In a rush she was at the stove rescuing the chicken. "All that butter," she muttered, "going up in smoke." The next moment she was blowing a gale into the speaking tube.

"What is it?" Elsie's voice shrilled from the mouthpiece.

Angela barked orders.

"But I'm busy, Angela, and anyway I don't see

why I'm always the one — "

"Lukewarm water, and no arguing." Angela snapped the speaking tube shut. "Up with them," she turned on Tom. "Be quick, but be careful. They're slippery when they're wet." On her way back to the stove, she patted the top of Tom's head. "I won't forget what you've done for me, and neither will the Lord," she said solemnly, "but be careful."

Tom and Elsie bathed the twins. Elsie, her face somewhat disfigured by splotches of paint and a resentful scowl, complained as she undressed Paul that she had had to stop painting in the middle and that all her work was probably ruined. However, the misery of the twins as they drooped in the bath water, slippery and whimpering, wrung pity even from Elsie.

"There, there," she murmured as she wiped the smears from Paul's face. "It was a mean old Angela to forget him. Mean, mean Angela."

"Heap reproaches on my head. They are as feathers compared to the heaviness of my own remorse." Angela loomed in the bathroom door. "Elsie Stackpole, don't you dare to lift that child with one hand. Use two."

Angela hovered over the tub until the twins were safely washed and dried. She pointed to their supper laid ready in the bedroom. "First give them a bottle, then the cereal and eggs, and then, if they've got the strength left to go on, give them another bottle. They need building up after all they've suffered." She wagged her forefinger at Tom and Elsie. "Be careful," she warned and hurried back to the kitchen.

Very carefully Tom and Elsie lowered themselves and their burdens into chairs. Each awkwardly propped a twin against one arm and poked a bottle into its slack and quivering mouth. Instantly the twins galvanized. Their lips clamped on the nipples. Their eyes glinted, and their chins worked with a firm stubborn motion as, in what seemed a single, mighty draught, they finished the milk and endeavored to suck in nipples and bottles as well. Elsie tugged her end of the bottle until it came loose with a pop and rolled away across the floor. Restored to vigor, Paul roared and waved his fists so wildly that he knocked the first spoonful of egg right out of Elsie's hand. Then, choking with rage and frustration, he turned purple and made his eyes bug out. Elsie slapped him on the back and retrieved the spoon. Roaring again and flailing his arms, he snapped wildly at the spoon.

"Pig," said Elsie, and now her chin set stubbornly and her eye glinted as with all her strength she forced Paul back into position, "since you're in such a hurry, I'll show you," and she began spooning egg into Paul at a murderous pace.

After a sharp struggle, Tom had got the empty

bottle away from Richard, only to have him seize the first spoonful of egg between his gums and hold on like a bulldog.

"Let go," begged Tom, "let go." He pried at the spoon. Richard hung on. "I can't get it out," wailed Tom. "He's too strong. He may eat it. What'll I do?"

"Just pull hard," advised Elsie. She was still spooning egg into Paul at a rate that even he was having trouble to keep up with. He coughed and spluttered. "You wanted to race," said Elsie somewhat vindictively, "so now we're racing."

"Race!" Tom yanked the spoon loose, and Richard bellowed. Tom disregarded him. His face brightened. "Elsie," he shouted above Richard's cries, "let's race them against each other."

Elsie stopped spooning. She smiled. "Tom, sometimes you have good ideas. We'll start with the cereal so it'll be fair."

"On your mark, get set, go!" shouted Tom a few minutes later.

Tom and Elsie spooned their hardest. The twins gagged and sputtered, and at intervals let forth enraged howls, but gradually they caught on. There was no time for displays of temper. Either they ate their fastest or they strangled. Paul won the cereal.

"Richard," said Tom judiciously, "wastes time on the spoon, but I'll break him of it."

"It's too bad," said Elsie as she reached for Paul's

second bottle, "that we didn't think of this sooner. I'll bet they set a record on that first bottle."

"On your mark, get set, go!" shouted Tom.

The twins attacked the bottles with spirit.

"Atta boy, Richard," cried Tom. "Come on. You can do it."

Elsie glanced hastily from Paul's bottle to Richard's. "Hurry, Paul, hurry!" She jiggled him up and down.

"Keep it up, Richard, you're winning!" Tom hunched down over his entry and, to his disgust, saw Richard's chin working more slowly, less surely. He gave him a sharp nudge. Richard jumped. His chin worked hard for a minute, only to slow down again and stop. His eyes had lost their greedy glint. They were glazed and contented. "He's going to sleep," Tom exploded in indignation, "and just when he was winning too. Richard!" He shook him. Richard grunted softly. His eyes closed. The bottle hung loose in Tom's hand. "Come on, Richard, don't give up now." Tom pressed the nipple into Richard's mouth, rubbed it against his gums, jiggled him, jerked him, and begged him to exert himself. Richard smiled in his sleep.

"It's no use," said Tom. "He's quit."

He turned to see how Elsie was doing. She was still poking the bottle at Paul, and milk was trickling from the corners of his sagging mouth. His eyes were closed, and he snored gently.

"Drat it," Elsie held up her half-empty bottle, "just when it was getting exciting too."

They compared bottles. Richard had won by half an ounce.

"I suppose that makes it a tie," said Elsie. "It's too bad we couldn't do two out of three." She set down her bottle and hiked the unconscious Paul onto her shoulder.

"If we could manage to feed them every night," Tom frowned thoughtfully at Richard, "we could have a sort of tournament."

Elsie jerked her pigtails. "We could keep a regular score. I could make a score card with their names and the dates and stick on stars for when they won. Oh Tom," her eyes danced, "do you suppose Angela would let us feed them every night?"

"It would be a help to her," said Tom. "It would be thoughtful of us."

"Come on." Elsie jumped up. "Let's put them to bed quick and ask her."

Angela accepted their offer to feed the twins with somber humility.

"I've been looking after you two for a good many years," she said as she mashed the potatoes, "and now that I'm getting too old and stupid to do my work, you'll help me like dutiful children."

"Oh Angela, you're not really so very old," said Elsie kindly, and she hurried Tom upstairs to help her make out the score card.

Dinner that evening, the first in the new house, should have been a happy occasion. Angela had set the dining-room table with the best silver and glassware, and it glowed and sparkled in the candlelight. The chicken was only a little burned. The vegetables and mashed potatoes were perfect, but Angela herself, serving the plates in a cloud of self-reproach, cast a blight on the company.

"The slaughter of the innocents," she muttered as she passed the gravy.

"But they weren't slaughtered," cried Mrs. Stackpole.

"The Lord intervened and snatched them away from his unworthy servant," replied Angela. "Otherwise they were as good as slaughtered."

"No, Angela," said Tom hastily, "you just forgot, and I just happened to — "

"Silence, child," replied Angela. "I am an unworthy servant, and you were the instrument of the Lord."

She stalked away into the kitchen. A minute later her steps were heard on the back stairs as she went up to look at the twins.

"I wish she'd stop," sighed Mrs. Stackpole. "We all forget things sometimes, and no harm was done. The twins are sleeping beautifully. Tom and Elsie are old enough now to wash and feed them, and I'm glad they offered to do it every night. Angela works too hard."

"I like to," said Elsie primly. "It's a change from working on the doll's house."

"I like to, too," put in Tom.

"What did you do all day?" Mr. Stackpole asked him.

"I started repairing the old boat I found," said Tom in what he hoped was an offhand manner.

Elsie eyed him sharply. "I don't believe you know enough to repair an old boat all by yourself," she said.

Tom wiggled uncomfortably, but at that moment Mr. Stackpole said, "Sh."

Everyone listened to Angela's footsteps descending the stairs.

"Eat up quickly," whispered Mr. Stackpole, "and when she comes back, all of you ask for second helpings. That may cheer her up."

Everyone asked for seconds, but Angela showed no sign of cheering up.

"They were sleeping like tops, weren't they, Angela?" Mr. Stackpole tried to rally her.

Angela nodded glumly.

"Missing a meal once in a while is good for them," Mr. Stackpole went on. "Now just forget about them and stop blaming yourself."

"I can't," said Angela. "If any harm comes to those lambs through my neglect, I shall walk right down to that river and throw myself in."

"Don't," exclaimed Tom. "You'll drown."

"Drowning," returned Angela, "is better than I deserve."

She swept the group with a glance of unmitigated gloom and retired. A minute later she could be heard ascending the stairs.

"We must do something," said Mr. Stackpole. "This is unbearable."

Mrs. Stackpole wrinkled her forehead. "If I were to sit down at the piano right after dinner and make her sing while I accompanied, do you think it would take her mind off her troubles? I could pick out cheerful hymns and steer her away from the sad ones."

"That's a good idea," cried Mr. Stackpole. He put down his fork and listened to be sure that Angela was still upstairs. "There's something I should tell all of you." He lowered his voice and put a finger to his lips. "The day I first saw the house and agreed to buy it, I did something else too. I went into the town and looked up the ministers of both the churches. I guess I should have spent the time looking into that real estate agent, Mr. What's-His-Name, but I wanted to be sure Angela would be happy here. That seemed more important at the time. I told the ministers about Angela being a strong church woman and having such a fine voice. I asked if they'd be interested in having her as a soloist." Mr. Stackpole leaned forward and his voice rose. "They both wanted to grab her up, sight unseen, just on my recommendation. Of course, I couldn't commit her to anything. Both the ministers are coming to call on her any day now. Each one seemed afraid the other would get her first." Angela's footsteps started down the stairs. "Don't tell her," hissed Mr. Stackpole. "I want it to be a surprise, and the more practice she gets in, the better." He finished with a triumphant smile at his wife.

"I'll make her practice," Mrs. Stackpole whispered back. "I'll have her singing anthems and cantatas. She's got the voice. I'll make a real soloist of her."

When first asked to sing, Angela refused flatly. Where music was concerned, however, Mrs. Stackpole was surprisingly forceful. She ordered Angela to the piano and started her off with "Christ the Lord Is Risen To-day." Angela sang off key and slid all over the Alleluias. Mrs. Stackpole scolded her and made her try again. Angela scowled, but obeyed and managed to hit all the notes.

"Now let's have some spirit in it," commanded Mrs. Stackpole. She bobbed her head and counted the beats.

By nine o'clock, when Tom and Elsie were sent to bed, Angela had warmed up on all the more stirring hymns in the book and was perspiring as she attacked a long and difficult oratorio. It was late before she and Mrs. Stackpole finally tore themselves from the oratorio and retired, humming, to their rooms. It was later still when the rasping sound followed by the thump resounded through the silent house.

Mr. Stackpole rolled over in his bed. "Forgot pump," he mumbled. "Remind tomorrow."

On the third floor Angela didn't wait for Elsie to call. "It's the pump again. Your daddy forgot about it. Go to sleep," she called into the darkness.

Her voice rang with authority. Elsie, hovering between sleep and terror, drew Paddy Paws under the blanket and went back to sleep.

THE NEXT MORNING Angela was quite herself again. She disposed of the twins and cooked pancakes for the rest of the family. She shooed Paddy Paws off the kitchen table. She told Buddy he was a hairy old slob and then let him lick syrup off the plates. She explained to Mrs. Stackpole the proper way to hold a paintbrush. She reminded Mr. Stackpole to get the pump fixed before he forgot again. She presented Tom with a packet of sandwiches and pie for lunch so he could eat down by his boat and not come in late and drop crumbs all over her kitchen.

"Now get along," she said patting him on the head. "It's late and I want to get after those diamond panes."

Tom departed with the sandwiches under his arm, Buddy at his heels, and his fishing line in his pocket. Down by the river he found Joe lying on his back. Joe grinned and waved a large paw in greeting.

"You're early," he said. "Gotta digest my breakfast. Sit down and rest."

"Gee," replied Tom, "Angela said it was late."

"That Angela," Joe yawned, "she don't give you a minute's peace. You sit down and forget about her and tell me the names of them pretty songs your ma was singin' last night. I've heard 'em before somewhere, but I can't exactly remember."

"That wasn't my mother," said Tom. "That was — " He stopped.

Joe rolled over and gave Tom a puzzled stare. "I was sure it was your ma," he said softly. "If it wasn't your ma, who was it?"

"I'm sorry, Joe," said Tom, "but it was Angela."

"Her!" Joe turned away again.

"She likes to sing hymns," Tom explained, "and my mother says she has a very good voice. I guess it must be good," he added, "for you to hear it way down here."

Joe got to his feet with unusual energy. "Let's haul down the boat," he said, "and go fishing."

When they tried to persuade Buddy to get in the boat, he sat down on the bank and stuck to it as if he were glued. However, as soon as they pushed off without him and the water widened between him and Tom, he bayed so mournfully that they had to come back and lift him aboard. He crouched in the bottom and fixed Tom with a reproachful, bloodshot stare until the sun and the gentle motion lulled him back to his usual state of torpor. Tom was delighted when Joe asked him if he wanted to row. They crossed to the far side of the river because Joe said there was less current there and more water between them and the new house that someone had built right close to the riverbank practically trespassing on the river.

"I suppose I got no right to complain," said Joe as Tom rowed steadily upstream and the new house, bright behind its shrubbery, slipped behind them, "but I kinda feel they ought've asked me before putting a house smack up against my river."

The river wound through woodland now, and while Tom sweated with the oars, Joe leaned back in the stern seat and smiled benignly over his domain.

"There's a kingfisher lives up here," he said. "I want you should see him dive, and there's redwings, and swallers all over the place, and muskrat, and some of the prettiest snakes." He stretched his legs and let one hand hang lazily in the water. "This is the life," he said.

About a mile upstream, they tied their boat to the end of a dead tree which had fallen out over the water. Joe baited the hooks with bacon (less trouble than digging worms, he explained) and they dropped the lines into the river. As the current tugged at his line Tom felt tugs of excitement in his stomach. He stared into the water and braced himself for the first bite. However, as the minutes passed without a bite, and the sun beat down, and Joe pointed out redwings and swallers or remarked that the old kingfisher was around somewhere, he could hear him rattling, Tom relaxed his vigilance. Imitating Joe, he reclined across the seat with his feet up. He watched with interest the struggles of two turtles to haul themselves onto the fallen tree for a sunbath. A snake slithered down the bank into the water.

"Snakes are pretty," commented Joe. "I'd have one for a pet if I was more settled. Birds don't like to be made pets of, but a snake don't mind."

"I'd like one too," Tom replied dreamily. "I'd take it to school in my pocket," and he fell into a day-dream about what he would do with a snake in school.

"There's old kingfisher," whispered Joe, "just above us. Now sit still, and maybe he'll dive."

The kingfisher perched motionless on a branch overhanging the river. With tousled head and thick beak, he looked like a concert pianist poised to strike the first chord. Tom and Joe waited motionless. Suddenly, like a stone, the kingfisher dropped head first into the river. He came up a minute later empty-billed and flapped off, rattling out his annoyance.

"Hey, look out!" Joe lunged forward, grabbing Tom's reel just as it was about to jump overboard and knocking Tom into the bottom of the boat. Joe hauled on the line. Buddy reared up, planted his front paws on Tom's chest, and licked his face. Loops of wet line wound themselves around Tom and Buddy, and then, with a plop, a large and struggling fish landed in Tom's face. Buddy recoiled and tried, in a series of elephantine leaps, to untangle himself and throw himself out of the boat. Joe bellowed, grabbed at the leaping fish, missed and fell across the seats. At the same moment Buddy succeeded in launching himself over the side. The boat heaved. A torrent of water poured into Tom's face. With a wild gesture of self-protection, he reached up to beat back the water. His hands closed on the fish. As the boat rocked and the water sloshed over him, he heard Joe shouting, "Hang on! Hang on!"

He hung on until, as the rocking of the boat subsided, Joe got his balance and relieved him of the now weak and gasping fish. Joe knocked its head against the side of the boat. It was a fine large bass.

"It's lucky for us he's so big," remarked Joe as he laid the fish out across the seat, "because it's gonna take the rest of the morning to untangle the lines, and I'd hate to disappoint you twice about lunch."

"I'm sorry," said Tom, "that Buddy and I made such a mess." He wrung the water from his pants and avoided looking at Joe, who sounded almost cross.

"It's nothing to feel sorry about so long as we got the fish, and that old Buddy, I guess he's just timid by nature." Joe broke into a rumbling chuckle, and Tom smiled at him in grateful relief.

Buddy, who could swim in a pinch and had made it to shore, now sat on the bank and watched while Tom and Joe bailed out the boat and untangled the lines. He whined apologetically at intervals, and Joe said such funny things about Buddy's character and how he was the kind of watchdog that held the lantern for you while you picked the lock that Tom shook with laughter. Getting Buddy back into the boat was another long and complicated operation. He couldn't quite summon enough courage to come aboard under his own power, although he indicated by all sorts of grunts and whines and tail wavings that his spirit was willing and he bore no grudges. Joe finally picked him up and deposited him in the boat.

While they drifted downstream, Joe cleaned the fish. Back at the camp site, Tom helped lay the fire, and when the coals were right Joe fried the fish in butter. He kept a supply in a jar which he set in the shallow water and moored to a stump on the bank. The fish smelled delicious as it sizzled and browned in the butter, but somehow, for such a large fish, it fried down awfully small. Tom noticed a sadness in Joe's face as he carefully turned the fish, and Tom felt with remorse that Joe's sadness had something to do with the smallness of the fish. Happily Tom remembered his packet of sandwiches. He had dropped them in the grass and forgotten all about them. They were still there.

"Joe," he cried. "I forgot that I brought some sandwiches for my lunch. You can eat the whole fish yourself."

"You did?" Joe looked up and all the sadness had left his face. "I never knew anyone to beat you for thoughtfulness." Tom hung his head modestly. "But I wouldn't think of eating all the fish away from you. No sir, we'll split the fish and the sandwiches, share and share alike. What kind of sandwiches?"

They ate fish and sandwiches, share and share alike, and drank some coffee left over from Joe's breakfast. The birds chirped in the surrounding trees, the oriole's note sounded occasionally from the woods, and Tom, when his mouth wasn't full, produced some first-rate imitations of it. When the sandwiches and fish were gone, there was still the pie.

"You can have it," said Tom. "I'm full."

"Are you sure, Tom? Are you sure you're full?" Joe's hand hovered over the pie. "Because it's a fair-ish piece, and if you ain't full — "

"I'm full, honest." Tom patted his stomach and stretched out on his back. Joe's hand closed on the pie.

Tom lay staring up at the treetops. He wanted to pick out another song from the medley of twitterings and learn to whistle it as well as he did the oriole's. He had listened a long time before he caught a trill like running water, more songlike, more beautiful than any of the other chirps and twitters. Tom stiffened and listened harder than ever. Again he caught the song, and with a rush of happiness knew he remembered it.

"Joe," he whispered and lay quite still for he knew better now than to jump up or shout and scare the bird away, "I hear the wood thrush."

Joe made no reply.

"There. There it is again. It is the wood thrush, isn't it?"

Still Joe said nothing, and very quietly Tom turned toward him. Joe was staring straight ahead. His forehead was puckered, and his lips curved in an expectant smile.

"That's it," Tom whispered as once more the song rose and fell.

Joe shook his head. "Can't get it," he muttered. "It don't come clear."

Tom was shocked at Joe's denseness. "There," he nudged Joe's arm, "it's nearby. We can creep close up."

"No," Joe mumbled, and shook his head as if it hurt him.

"But we did yesterday. Remember? You remember, Joe. You must remember."

Suddenly, with a scream, the blue jay swooped across the clearing.

Joe ducked his head down between his knees, and Tom saw, to his astonishment, that Joe was trembling. Tom forgot the thrush and stared at Joe wondering why he was suddenly so queer.

"Do you feel all right?" Tom asked after a minute.

Slowly Joe raised his head and examined a mangled scrap of pie he still held in his hand.

"Where'd you get this pie?" He turned to Tom.

Tom sighed. He hated to mention Angela again, especially now when Joe seemed to feel queer. "Didn't you like it?" he asked.

Joe looked hard at the pie. "Like it!" He rolled his eyes and licked his lips. He seemed to be feeling better. "I been trying to remember when I ever tasted pie as good as this, but then I remembered something else." He scowled at the pie and started to throw it away. "No," he checked his throw, "couldn't be." He put the pie in his mouth, chewed thoughtfully and swallowed it.

"Your ma make it?" he asked in his usual friendly way.

"Well, no."

"Then who did?"

Tom sighed again. "Angela," he admitted.

"Her," snorted Joe and scowled down at his feet.

"The wood thrush is gone," ventured Tom to change the subject. "I guess the jay scared him away."

"Did you hear a wood thrush?" Joe asked.

"Yes, it was nearby. Didn't you hear it?"

"I guess your ears are gettin' sharper than mine." Joe rubbed his head. "Let's try some more fishing." He got to his feet and started toward the boat.

All the afternoon they fished, with Buddy asleep in the bottom of the boat and no mishaps. When the sun hanging low over the marsh became uncomfortably hot, they drifted home while Joe cleaned the two pickerel they had caught for his supper and coached Tom in his attempts to whistle the song of the red-winged blackbird. At the camp they swam again in the rushing current then lay on the bank and loafed until, as the sun began to disappear behind the marsh, Joe became restive.

"String beans," he muttered, "lettuce and tomatoes." He smacked his lips and stood up. "I guess you'd better be getting home," he said, and turning toward his duffel bag he murmured softly, "fresh eggs, soft-boiled."

At the mention of soft-boiled eggs Tom got up too. "I've gotta feed the twins. Angela'll be awful mad if I'm late."

"That woman," grunted Joe, "ought to be a drill sergeant." He shook himself and turned to Tom. "See you tomorrow," he grinned. "Tomorrow I'll bet you catch another big bass."

"I'll try." Tom grinned back and trotted toward home.

WHEN TOM REACHED the clothesyard, the twins hailed him with whoops of joy. Richard even hauled himself to his feet and balanced triumphantly for a minute before his legs gave way and he toppled over. Tom gathered up both twins and carried them gurgling into the kitchen.

"Here they are," he announced, "and there's nothing wrong with them tonight."

He inhaled the cooking smells and grinned at Angela who was bent over the oven. Angela straightened herself.

"The Lord is merciful," she murmured, and burst into "O Worship the King."

Paul won on the egg, but Richard won both the cereal and the bottle. Elsie took defeat in a sporting manner and, without so much as a grumble, pasted two gold stars after Richard's name.

"I've finished the outside painting," she announced at dinner, "and if I do say so, it looks marvelous, just like the big house, only better."

"I wish I could say the same for the ceiling," said Mr. Stackpole, and he rubbed his neck.

"What did the man say about the pump?" Angela paused above the dish of spinach she was passing.

"He fixed it," said Mr. Stackpole more cheerfully. "There was nothing really wrong. He just oiled it. He said that if we had any more noises to call him and he'd take a look at the furnace. Might be the hot-water system."

"Good." Angela gave him an approving nod. "I'm glad you didn't forget. I finished the third-floor windows, six hundred and forty panes. Professional cleaners, hah!" She returned to the kitchen, and the strains of "Rise, Crowned with Light" reverberated through the door.

"I should think she'd be tired," exclaimed Mrs. Stackpole. "I've painted half a ceiling and I can hardly move."

"Go right to bed," admonished Mr. Stackpole. "Don't stay up playing for Angela. You'll get even lamer, and we've got at least two more coats to go."

"I hate to disappoint her," said Mrs. Stackpole.

"Mrs. Stackpole," said Angela when she returned with the peach shortcake, "you go right to bed. You're too lame to play the piano."

"Well, Angela, I guess I will."

"And the rest of you too," continued Angela, "let's all get a good night's sleep for once."

That night there were no noises and everyone did get a good night's sleep.

For Tom the next few weeks were the happiest he had ever known. The lazy late summer days slipped by as serenely as the river itself while together with Joe he fished and swam and watched the birds and animals.

Poling the boat far into the marsh and wading knee-high in mud, Tom searched out the nests of red-wings, swamp sparrows, and warblers. Sitting perfectly still in the boat he saw a muskrat swimming to his house of piled-up reeds at the edge of the marsh. With Joe's help he learned to know all the common bird songs and to whistle some of them quite creditably. The jay, the oriole, and the fussy little wren visited often in the clearing and came to seem like old friends. The notes of the wood thrush rippling from the woods lured Tom and Joe on daily sorties into the underbrush. Creeping noiselessly and crouching motionless they watched the thrush with his speckled breast pulsing in song, and Tom learned in time to whistle his notes. On the river the kingfisher fished along with them, and his luck varied much as their own did. Joe was always easy and good-natured. When Tom fell flat on his face in the mud while he was trying to catch a snake, Joe rinsed his clothes in the river and laid them out to dry. Tom knew, although her name was not mentioned, that Joe went to this trouble to protect him from the wrath of Angela. When they ate their lunches of fish or frogs' legs (Tom came in time to be fond of frogs' legs), supplemented by sandwiches and a piece of cake or pie, Tom saw to it that Joe got most of the cake or pie. Joe ate these delicacies with a faraway, almost ecstatic expression on his broad black face. For a long time after he had finished he sat perfectly still, his brow faintly puckered, his lips curved in the beginning of a smile. When Joe was in this state, Tom was very careful not to disturb him or remind him in any way of the source of the baked goods which transported him into such a blissful stupor.

At home, in the evenings, life was pleasant too. The twins were running neck and neck. Angela had come to regard the old house with its acres of floor and innumerable diamond panes as a worthy opponent for her own superior abilities. After a hard day's cleaning, she took pride in cooking superb dinners just to show the house that it wasn't too much for her. Toward Tom and Elsie she was unusually gentle. She still seemed to regard them as Instruments of the Lord. Since they had undertaken the evening feeding, the twins, according to Angela, were thriving as never before. They left not so much as a crumb of their supper uneaten, they slept like angels, and were the handsomest, best-natured, and most intelligent babies in the world. When Angela, towering above some steaming dish and looking like a benign genie in

the candlelight, held forth on the virtues of the Stackpole children, Tom wished that Joe could hear her.
He'd see for himself that she wasn't just bossy. She
was good and kind and understanding as well.

Every night, at dinner Elsie reported on her progress with the doll's house. Her parents listened with
interest, for they were encountering very similar
problems in the redecoration of the living room. Conversation revolved for the most part around priming
coats, spackle, gloss, semigloss, varnish, woodseal, and
methods for removing old wallpaper (there were
four layers in the living room). Sometimes Mr. and
Mrs. Stackpole remembered to ask Tom how he was
coming with his boat, but their enthusiasm for the
house and their own work kept them from taking a
very deep interest. When asked, Tom simply answered, "Fine," and let it go at that. Elsie's troubles
with Paddy Paws received more attention. Paddy
Paws had taken up residence in the living room of
the doll's house and was obviously planning to give
birth to her next batch of kittens there.

"I don't know what I'm going to do," complained
Elsie. "Paddy growls and scratches when I just
reach in with the putty knife."

Mr. Stackpole laughed. "Well, Laura, that's one
problem we don't have, thank heavens."

Tom, who slept soundly after his days on the river,
forgot all about the pump and its curious noises, but
it still kicked up sometimes. Mr. and Mrs. Stackpole

and Angela heard it when they went to bed late after a session of hymn singing. The screech or rasp followed by the thud half wakened Elsie, and Paddy did the rest. Paddy, who was nervous these days, always leaped from the doll's house to Elsie's bed where she paced back and forth emanating electric shocks like a charged battery. Each time this happened it was Angela who had to come to the rescue and convince Elsie that it was just the pump, not a ghost. She became understandably annoyed.

"Mr. Stackpole," she commanded, "you call that pump man in again and this time see to it that he does something."

CHAPTER 10

TOM PICKED UP the twins one evening a little later than usual. They kicked and whinnied like a couple of impatient race horses and Tom hurried them to the kitchen. He needn't have hurried, as it turned out. Elsie had walked to town to do some errands for Angela and she was not yet back.

"Sit down and wait," said Angela comfortably, "while I finish my cake. I sent Elsie on purpose because she needs exercise and air. She's pale as a sheep, and her neck's all crooked from twisting around in that doll's house. Put the twins on the floor. It's clean. They'll like to crawl around a little." Angela set down her spoon and got two crusts of bread. "There," she said, handing a crust to each twin, "you sharpen your teeth on these until Elsie comes."

Mrs. Stackpole began to play the piano softly in the front of the house. Angela poured melted chocolate into the mixture in her bowl and stirred in time to the music. The twins gnawed on the crusts, and Tom, grateful for Angela's gentle mood and a chance to rest, leaned back in a kitchen chair and breathed

99

in the fragrance of the chocolate. Angela talked on as she worked, partly to Tom, partly to herself.

"She's stopped in at the library most likely and forgotten the time. The Lord gave her brains, and there's a lot to be learned from books by those who have brains." Angela nodded sagely at her batter. "For those without brains," Angela added a little milk, "the Lord provides otherwise, and it's best not to interfere." She sifted flour into the batter and mixed it thoroughly. "I have brains," she went on, "and little Elsie has brains, and Mr. Stackpole, I suppose, has brains of a sort. The others — " She clucked her tongue and shook her head. "But," she poured in more milk and stirred again, "the Lord gave them virtues He denied to the ones with brains. Take my Eddy." She stopped stirring and looked off dreamily. "Eddy had no brains to speak of, but that didn't prevent him being a hero, and I shouldn't have made him study his books so hard or nagged at him so much. He was good enough the way the Lord made him. He was a hero, and I'd no right to interfere." She sighed and turned back to her beating. Softly she began to hum "By Cool Siloam's Shady Rill."

While she talked Tom had been dreaming about Joe and the river. He smiled now as he recognized the tune. It fitted pleasantly with his own thoughts.

"When are you going to take me to ride in that boat of yours?"

100

Tom stiffened, then hanging his head he muttered, "Haven't finished working on it."

"I told you it would take a lot of fixing," said Angela. "Didn't think you'd have the patience to keep at it so long. I must go down and have a look at what you've done."

Tom swallowed. "No," he shook his head, "I mean you wouldn't want to go down there now. It's all grown up with brambles. You couldn't get through."

Angela squared her shoulders. "Do I look like one who couldn't get through a few brambles?"

Tom could think of nothing to say in reply. He knew, although he didn't dare look at her, that Angela was eying him curiously.

"What reason have you got for not wanting me to go down there?" she asked.

The kitchen door burst open.

"I'm sorry I'm late," panted Elsie. "I've run all the way. I've had the most exciting time." She dumped her bundles on the table. "I bet you can't guess where I've been."

"I think I can," Angela smiled.

"Where?"

"The library."

"Oh Angela," Elsie tossed her pigtails, "you're too omniscient."

Angela chuckled.

"But," Elsie continued, "you don't know what I've found out."

Angela shook her head.

"I've found out all about this house. The librarian told me, and she knows because her grandmother told her, and she's very nice. I mean the librarian, and she said I was unusual for my age, and just wait till you hear about it." Elsie's eyes snapped.

Angela raised her hand. "I want to hear about it, but first you take care of your twin. You can tell us all about it at dinner."

As soon as everyone was seated at the table, Elsie launched forth. "This house was built in 1850 by a gentleman named Amos Follonsbee who was a little ec-ec — well, he was a little queer in the head."

"Who said he was queer in the head?" asked Mr. Stackpole.

"Miss Chapin's grandmother," returned Elsie. "He got all excited about new ideas and hadn't a notion of the value of money, and, well, he built this house."

"I don't see how that follows," interrupted Mr. Stackpole.

"Miss Chapin says that no one who wasn't — you know," Elsie tapped her forehead, "would build a house that looked like this and just ate up money besides. She says heating it in winter runs well into four figures."

"Oh, she does, does she?"

"Yes, she says the house has always been called Follonsbee's Folly. She's very anxious to meet you."

Mr. Stackpole fidgeted with his fork.

"That's very interesting, dear," Mrs. Stackpole nodded at Elsie, "because the pump man came about the noise again this afternoon, and what was it he said about the furnace, Richard? I'm afraid I was busy and didn't pay attention."

Mr. Stackpole looked his wife straight in the eye. "He said we needed a whole new heating system."

"Well now," Mrs. Stackpole smiled, "I guess that's been the trouble ever since 1850."

Mr. Stackpole braced himself in his chair. "Installing the new system will take every penny that's left of Aunt Elsie's legacy, and the oil bill will still run well into four figures."

"Oh dear," Mrs. Stackpole's forehead wrinkled, "you didn't tell me that."

Mr. Stackpole dabbed at his mouth with his napkin. "Well, now you know."

"But the noise in the night," Elsie burst in, "will still go on." She glanced into the dim corners of the room and shuddered.

Angela emerged from the shadows near the kitchen door. She was still carrying the dish of string beans with which she had started for the kitchen. "Elsie Stackpole, what new foolishness is this?"

"It's not foolishness," retorted Elsie. "It's what

Miss Chapin heard from her grandmother, and she knew."

"Tell it," said Angela grimly. She drew up a chair and sat down with the beans in her lap.

"I'm trying to," sputtered Elsie, "but you all keep interrupting."

"I'm sorry," sighed Mr. Stackpole. "What else did Miss Chapin say?"

"Mr. Follonsbee was an ec-ec-eccentric widower," Elsie smiled in triumph, "with one little girl. He loved the little girl very much. With his own hands he built a little round summerhouse down by the river for the little girl to play in, and Miss Chapin's grandmother used to be invited to play with her. They played dolls in the summerhouse."

"It's still there," Tom burst in. "I've seen it often," he added with a feeling of importance.

"You have?" Elsie turned on him. "Miss Chapin wondered if there was any of it left. Her grandmother said it used to be very beautiful."

Tom's feeling of importance gave way to alarm as he realized that it would be just like Elsie to invite Miss Chapin to come and see the summerhouse.

"It's not beautiful any more," he said. "It's all broken down and covered with brambles. There's nothing much to see. It's a wreck."

"Too bad," said Elsie. "Now where was I?"

"Miss Chapin's grandmother played dolls with Mr. Follonsbee's little girl," Mr. Stackpole reminded her, "and if I may say so, Elsie, you still haven't explained why Mr. Follonsbee was considered so eccentric or why the noise will go on."

"I'm coming to that." Elsie licked her lips. "Once Miss Chapin's grandmother was asked to spend the night. In the middle of the night she was waked up by creakings and footsteps and low voices. She was scared, and she began to cry, but no one came to comfort her because Mr. Follonsbee only kept one servant, and she went home at night, and Mr. Follonsbee didn't hear her either. She cried harder and harder until she woke up Althea Follonsbee, her little friend. Althea told Miss Chapin's grandmother to stop crying. The noises happened often and had something to do with Mr. Follonsbee's business. Althea went back to sleep, but Miss Chapin's grandmother didn't sleep a wink the rest of the night." Elsie flipped her pigtails, and her eyes swept triumphantly over the absorbed faces of her listeners.

"Miss Chapin's grandmother would never spend another night in this house," continued Elsie. "It was too scary, but she still came in the daytime. Althea had lovely toys, and Miss Chapin's grandmother felt sorry for her being an only child and living so far from town. Mostly they played in the summerhouse by the river. They took picnic lunches, and sometimes Mr. Follonsbee came down and ate his lunch with them, and he was just as nice as anything."

"Of course he was," said Mr. Stackpole. "He was a man of imagination, and he employed a good architect."

"No one ever said he wasn't nice, Daddy, but he was eccentric and wild with his money. Now listen. After he'd built the big house and all, he sent Althea off to an expensive boarding school in Boston and lived here all alone. He said he wanted her to learn music and French and embroidery, but there was a perfectly good school for young ladies right here in Carlton where Miss Chapin's grandmother learned everything she needed to know, and if that wasn't extravagant, well, Miss Chapin would like to know what was. Besides even when Mr. Follonsbee was living all by himself, his orders from the butcher and the grocer were as big as if he'd been feeding an army. He kept the whole house heated too even though it was a very cold winter. When people asked him what he did with so much food and firewood, he laughed and said it all went underground. In Carlton it was generally thought that he was losing what mind he'd had." Elsie tossed her head at her father. "When Althea came home for the long summer vacation, guess what she found as a surprise?" Elsie drew a deep breath. "The doll's house! The same doll's house I'm fixing up now. Althea and Miss Chapin's grandmother played with it. Just think, the doll's house has been here in the house for over a hundred years." Elsie's eyes sparkled and she hurried on before anyone could interrupt her. "Miss Chapin said she couldn't understand why it was still in the house, but I told her why."

"Why?" demanded Angela.

"Because," replied Elsie, "it's too big to fit through the door or the window."

"Glory be," exclaimed Angela, "the child's right."

"The furniture for the doll's house is gone though," said Elsie sadly. "Miss Chapin's grandmother said it was all full of beautiful furniture just like Mr. Follonsbee's furniture in the big house. Even when Miss Chapin's grandmother was an old, old lady, she remembered the beautiful doll's house and the furniture, and she loved to tell her grandchildren about it. I wish — " began Elsie.

"To think," put in Mr. Stackpole, "that Mr. Follonsbee took all that trouble to build a doll's house and furnish it for his little girl. What a clever, kind-hearted man he must have been."

"He didn't build it," declared Elsie.

"You said he lived alone, and the doll's house won't fit through the door."

"Ah," replied Elsie mysteriously.

"If he didn't," demanded Angela, "then who did?"

"Guess!" With a superior smile Elsie challenged her listeners. "Angela," she teased, "you should be able to guess."

Angela's brows drew together in concentration. The candlelight cast unfamiliar shadows over her bony features. "I can't guess," she declared after a minute's fierce thought.

"Fugitive slaves built it. One of them might have been your ancestor, Angela." Elsie giggled. "There, now I've given it away."

"My ancestor!" Angela rose to her feet. Her eyes flashed at Elsie over the dish of string beans. "My ancestors, one and all," she proclaimed, "lived and died peaceful British subjects on the beautiful island of Barbados, where, if the Lord had not seen fit to chastise me with a worthless husband, I would be still today. My ancestors weren't racketing around the wilds of North America. They were growing their own vegetables and going to church regularly."

Elsie wilted under this blast. "I'm sorry, Angela. I just thought maybe."

"My ancestors!" Angela exploded again.

"Well, maybe your husband's ancestors," Elsie put in timidly.

"No Gittens ever left Barbados. They were too lazy. It was all they could do to get out of bed in the morning. That was why I left. I wanted to better myself and Eddy." Angela turned on Elsie. "You leave my ancestors alone. And don't you mix them up in the internal squabbles of a foreign land. We were nobody's slaves. We were loyal British subjects." Angela lifted her chin and glared out over the heads of the Stackpoles, who sat very still, ready to leap respectfully to their feet in case she was moved to sing "God Save the King."

Tom broke the expectant silence. "Who did make the doll's house, Elsie?"

"Don't you know?"

Tom shook his head, and Elsie perked up.

"You should know from what you've had of American History, but I'll tell you anyway. The doll's house was built by fugitive slaves who were escaping to freedom in Canada. This house was a station on the Underground Railroad. See?" Tom's eyes widened. "I knew quite a lot about it from school," said Elsie, "but Miss Chapin told me even more that her grandmother told her."

Tom rubbed his forehead. There had been something about that in school. He tried to think and remember, but it got all mixed up with spelling and fractions.

"Before the American Civil War," Elsie went on, and she emphasized American with a nod at Angela, "there were a lot of people in the North who thought slavery was so wicked that any slave who wanted to run away from his master should be helped to do it. These people didn't even care that it was against the law to help slaves run away from their masters. They did it secretly. They arranged for the runaway slaves to travel at night with guides and to sleep during the day in the houses of people who wanted to help them. There were regular escape routes, some by land and some by water, all the way from the Southern States to Canada. The river here was part of one of these routes, and Mr. Follonsbee took in escaping slaves and fed them in his house. That first winter when Althea was sent to boarding school was very cold. The river froze so you couldn't travel on it. A group of slaves had to stay here in the house all winter until the river thawed out in the spring. Mr. Follonsbee was very good to them, and they were comfortable and happy and grateful to Mr. Follonsbee. They built the doll's house and the furniture to thank him for his kindness. See?" Elsie stopped for breath.

Tom nodded, but he was still puzzled. He couldn't remember when the Civil War happened. He felt it was a long time ago, but he couldn't be sure. There'd been so many wars. Joe, camping down by the river, made it all the more mixed up. Joe was like a fugitive slave, the way he was so grateful for the sandwiches and pie and cake and let Tom row the boat and share his fish. It seemed almost as if Joe must be connected with all the things Elsie had been telling. Tom felt as if he should tell about Joe and show that he knew some things that Elsie didn't. One glance at Angela, however, still fierce and offended, and Tom remembered that he'd promised not to mention Joe to anyone in his family. It was silly to try to know as much as Elsie, anyway. Elsie always turned out to know more.

"You explain very well, Elsie," said Mr. Stackpole. "How did Miss Chapin's grandmother learn all this?"

111

"She didn't learn about it until the Civil War was over, and the slaves were all freed. By then Mr. Follonsbee had died bankrupt, and she and Althea were grown up. Althea told her, but she made her promise not to tell anyone else."

"So she went right ahead and told anyway?" demanded Mr. Stackpole indignantly. "She was a fine friend. I prefer Amos Follonsbee, eccentricity and all."

"No, Daddy," Elsie slapped her hand down on the table. "I wish you wouldn't leap at conclusions."

"I'm sorry," said Mr. Stackpole. "Go on."

"The rest of the story is about Althea," Elsie sighed. "When Mr. Follonsbee died, Althea hadn't any money at all, just the house with a lot of mortgages. She tried to earn money by giving lessons in piano and French and embroidery."

"Poor Althea," murmured Mrs. Stackpole.

"Yes," continued Elsie, "she never had many pupils. She was too proud and particular. When the pupils weren't any good, she refused to waste her time on them. When people said anything about her father's having been eccentric and extravagant or called the house Follonsbee's Folly, she flew into a rage and called them awful names. Miss Chapin's grandmother was her only friend, and she was the only one Althea ever told about the Underground Railroad. She wouldn't lower herself to explain to anyone else. Miss Chapin's grandmother got married at about this time, and she moved away for a while. If she'd been around to advise Althea, Althea wouldn't have done what she did, which was," Elsie drew breath, "to marry a man whom nobody knew anything about except that he was no good. She sold the house and went West with him. Before she left she told people that in three years she and her husband would be back, and they'd be so rich that they'd buy back the house and the whole town too, if they felt like it. Althea didn't come back in three years," said Elsie after a pause. "Miss Chapin's grandmother knew then that Althea hadn't got rich and would never come back. She was too proud. It wasn't until then that Miss Chapin's grandmother told other people about how Amos Follonsbee had used all his money to help the fugitive slaves. She hoped they'd understand better about Althea and her pride and her temper."

"Well, well," said Mr. Stackpole, "I begin to have some respect for Miss Chapin's grandmother."

"Miss Chapin says that her grandmother's explaining didn't do any good," Elsie shook her head. "Half the people said that Althea had made the story up, and the others said it just proved that Amos Follonsbee was queer in the head. Miss Chapin says that Althea had insulted just about everybody in town before she left."

113

"Poor Althea," murmured Mrs. Stackpole.

"And now," said Elsie, "we come to the spooky part and the noise."

"Yes?" Mr. Stackpole leaned forward.

Angela made a disapproving sound in her throat, but he paid no attention.

"A long time went by, and most people forgot about Althea. Miss Chapin's grandmother had settled in Carlton for good, and she had three children and was very happy, but she still remembered Althea and missed her. She wrote some letters to the town out west where Althea had said she was going, but the letters all came back. Miss Chapin's grandmother could never find out anything about Althea, where she lived, or if she was still alive. The people who'd bought this house from Althea had moved away because they'd lost all their money, and the house was up for sale and beginning to fall apart. Miss Chapin's grandmother often walked out to it with her children.

"Miss Chapin's mother, who lived to be ninety-eight (Miss Chapin's family is very robust), remembered these walks, and she's the one who told Miss Chapin the rest of the story. Miss Chapin's mother and her little brothers used to play hide-and-seek near the summerhouse until they were hot and tired. Then they were allowed to wade along the edge of the river, but not far out because the current was swift and they couldn't swim. After that, Miss Chapin's grandmother would take some apples and cookies out of her bag, and they'd have a picnic in the summerhouse while Miss Chapin's grandmother told them stories about the picnics she had had there with Althea when she was a little girl. Doesn't it sound lovely?" Elsie smiled. "I must go down and look at that summerhouse. Miss Chapin would like to go too."

"Listen, Elsie," Tom burst in. "It isn't lovely any more. It's all busted, and you and Miss Chapin couldn't break through the brambles. They're terrible. They'd cut you to ribbons."

"I don't believe it," returned Elsie, "and anyway Miss Chapin is very robust."

"Well, I'm warning you."

"I wish you'd stop interrupting," snapped Elsie. "We wouldn't come near you and your leaky old boat. We'd just sit in the summerhouse and remember the past."

"You can't sit in it," Tom protested angrily. "It's all busted."

"All right, we'd sit near it then. Are you going to let me go on with the story, or aren't you?"

Tom gave up. "Go on," he said.

"Miss Chapin's mother loved to hear about Althea and her toys and especially the doll's house. She wanted to break into the house and see if the doll's house was still there. Of course she wasn't allowed to, but she was allowed to peek in the downstairs windows of the house. Before they started home she always ran around the house, looking in each room and trying to imagine how it had been when it was all new and furnished, and Althea and her father lived there with the fugitive slaves hiding around in the corners." Elsie cast a quick glance around the corners of the dining room. "One day," she lowered her voice to a whisper, "Miss Chapin's mother saw something hanging over the banister at the foot of the front stairs. It had never been there before. It looked like a lady's bonnet and shawl and reticule. She heard a noise too, a sort of rasping noise and then a thump." Elsie cast another quick glance around the room and hurried on. "She ran to tell her mother who was walking in the old garden picking a few flowers. Her mother called the boys and hurried them all across the fields to the road. She said a prospective buyer must have come to look at the house, and she didn't want to be seen trespassing even though she wasn't doing any harm.

"They didn't walk to the house again for over a week. When they did go the For Sale sign was still up, so they had their picnic as usual, and Miss Chapin's mother peeked in the windows. The bonnet and shawl and reticule were still hanging on the banister. This time Miss Chapin's mother made Miss Chapin's grandmother come and look. Miss Chapin's grandmother looked, and then, because she had a funny feeling that something was wrong, she knocked at the door. No one answered the knock.

Miss Chapin's grandmother tried the door, and it opened. She stepped into the hall. It was all dim and cobwebby, just the way it was when we first came. Miss Chapin's grandmother called loudly, 'Is anyone there?' Her voice echoed back from the empty rooms. She took Miss Chapin's mother by the hand, and they went through every cupboard and closet in the house. They even opened the doll's house and looked inside. There was no trace of anyone. When they came back to the front hall, Miss Chapin's grandmother looked over the bonnet and shawl, and then she opened the reticule. She took out the things inside and laid them out on the stairs. There was a little money, the stub of a railroad ticket from Boston to Carlton, a big brass key, and a handkerchief with the initials A.F.T. embroidered in a wreath of flowers in one corner. Miss Chapin's grandmother picked up the handkerchief and her hands began to tremble. She looked hard at those embroidered initials and the wreath of flowers. Then, because she was shaking so and the light was dim, she carried it outside and steadied herself against the door while she looked at them again. The name of the man Althea had married was Tinkham, but it wasn't just because of that that Miss Chapin's grandmother left her little girl standing in the hall and ran all through the house again calling 'Althea, Althea, it's Grace. Answer me!' Miss Chapin's grandmother was no fool. She knew that lots of people have A.F.T. for initials, but she knew too that no one but Althea could have embroidered those flowers so neatly, so daintily, with such tiny, even stitches. After Miss Chapin's grandmother had been through the house the second time, she ran all over the yard and down to the summerhouse, calling and calling until it began to get dark. At last she gave up and took the children home.

"She couldn't sleep that night. First thing next morning she went to see the man who was agent for selling the house and asked him if a woman in a dark bonnet and shawl had come to get the key from him and look at the house. He said no one had so much as asked about the house. The key had been hanging on its hook in his office for months and was still hanging there. Miss Chapin's grandmother made the agent go to the house with her and look at the bonnet and shawl and the reticule. They searched the house and grounds again, but found no trace of anyone's having been there. They took the clothes to the stationmaster at Carlton station and asked him if he remembered if anyone dressed in them had got off the train from Boston on that day, over a week ago, when the little girl first saw the clothes and heard the noise inside the house. The stationmaster thought hard and said yes, he guessed there had been a woman dressed in clothes like that who got off the 11.55. Not many strangers got off the train at Carlton, and he'd noticed her because she had jumped to the platform real quick and hadn't asked her way or got in the cab that met the train. The cab driver remembered her too. He'd called out, 'Want a ride, lady?' and she'd brushed right past him as if she didn't hear. They asked people who lived along the road from the station if they remembered seeing a strange lady in a dark bonnet and shawl walking by at about noon on that day. A boy who'd been coming home from fishing remembered passing a lady on the road. He remembered, he said, because she smiled at him, and her face was white and haggard, and, and," Elsie gave a little shriek, "like the face of a ghost! Oh dear," she wailed, "I'm not afraid in the daylight, but at night — " She sucked in her breath.

"Don't be silly, Elsie," said Mr. Stackpole. "There must be some explanation."

"No, there isn't. No one ever found out if it was really Althea or if it was her ghost. That's how the house got its bad name."

"What bad name?"

"It's supposed to be haunted by Althea, and everyone who moves into it gets terribly poor just the way the Follonsbees did."

"That's absurd," cried Mr. Stackpole. "I hope Miss Chapin doesn't believe that."

"She didn't used to," said Elsie. "She used to think the people who lived in it got poor because the house gobbles up money. It's not practical. It's the whim of an unbalanced intellect. It's Follonsbee's Folly. She used to think that, and she's very anxious

119

to meet you, Daddy, but now," Elsie's eyes glowed like coals in her white face, "since I told her about the noise in the night, Miss Chapin doesn't know what to think." Elsie shuddered and buried her face in her hands.

"Elsie," said Angela in a solemn voice, "look at me."

"Yes, Angela."

I'm going to tell you something I've never told to anyone else, and you must believe me because what I'm telling is true, and it happened to me, not my grandmother." Angela bit her lower lip as if she were in pain. She took a deep breath, fixed her eyes on Elsie, and went on steadily. "Right after Eddy was killed, I wanted more than anything in the world to talk to him just once more and tell him how much I loved him and how my nagging and scolding didn't mean anything except that I was too ambitious and overbearing. I wanted to tell him I was sorry that I drove him to running away and enlisting. I felt that if I couldn't tell him, and if I couldn't hear him answer that he forgave me, I'd go crazy." Angela's eyes never wavered from Elsie's. "I went to spiritualists, people who claim to be able to call back the spirits of the dead. I'm ashamed now, but I went to a lot of them, one after the other. I paid them good money, and I asked them to call back Eddy's ghost so I could talk to him just once more. Those spiritualists were all alike. They took my money. They turned down the lights. They fell flat on their backs on the floor, and they moaned and groaned and foamed at the mouth. They fixed towels so they looked to be flying through the air, and they told me things Eddy's ghost was supposed to be saying. I wanted to believe. I tried to believe those words were coming from Eddy, but, so help me," Angela's voice rose, "there wasn't one thing any of them told me that could have come from Eddy. I knew Eddy. I knew how he talked. I knew how his mind ran. What they said wasn't even like him. Every bit of it was lies they made up to fool me. If Eddy'd been a ghost and could have come back, he'd have come to comfort me. Eddy was a good boy. He'd have come to me in my sorrow. He didn't come. From that I know that there's no such thing as ghosts, and anyone who says there is is lying."

As Angela finished speaking and leaned earnestly toward Elsie, an unearthly howl broke forth from the kitchen. Everyone leaped to his feet. The string beans clattered to the floor. Frozen in terror, all eyes fixed on the kitchen door as it swung slowly open, and Paddy Paws glided into the room. She made straight for the spilled beans, sniffed them, and yowled again. She had been waiting for her scraps, which had not arrived on schedule. She disliked beans. She was affronted.

121

There was no singing that night. Mrs. Stackpole
accompanied Elsie to her room and read soothing
stories aloud to her until she fell asleep with the light
on. Whistling defiantly Mr. Stackpole retreated to
the library where he added up sums. Angela fed
Paddy Paws, picked up the beans, washed the dishes,
and climbed to her room. There she sat, reading her
Bible, ready, if the noise should come, to go at once
to Elsie. The night wore on without disturbance.
It was well past midnight before Angela closed her
Bible, snapped off Elsie's light, and went to bed.

CHAPTER 11

THE NEXT MORNING was unusually hot and bright. Sun poured through the clean diamond panes, flooding the rooms with hot white light. There wasn't so much as a shadowy corner for a ghost to call his own.

"Elsie," said Mr. Stackpole, patting her shoulder, "your Miss Chapin should write mystery thrillers and publish them. Her flights of fancy deserve a larger public. Now Laura," he turned in a businesslike manner to his wife, "you go right ahead with the wallpaper. I'm going to telephone an engineer I know and get his opinon on the furnace. I don't think that fellow yesterday knew what he was talking about." He finished his breakfast and rose with an air of great efficiency.

"I," announced Angela with even greater efficiency, "am going to oil the hinges on every door in this house. There's not a one that hangs straight, and all the hinges are rusty. It's no wonder we hear noises with the doors flapping in every draft and the hinges all squeaking."

123

"I thought you said it was the pump," quavered Elsie.

"Stop fussing," boomed Angela. "Whatever it is, we'll get it." She rolled up her sleeves.

Tom set out for the river with his usual sandwiches and an enormous piece of chocolate cake. If any one of Angela's masterpieces of cookery could be picked out and set above all the rest, it was her chocolate cake. The sight of it, dark, fragrant, enriched with a whole pound of butter, and quite untouched because, during last night's foolishness, she had completely forgotten to serve it, was more than she could bear.

"I can't stand to see it sitting around," she said. "If you make yourself sick, you'll at least have got some pleasure out of it first, and it's no more wasted than going stale in the cake box. I thank the Lord that you have a good appetite. The rest of this family can't be counted on, and the twins are too young." With a flourish of the oil can, she waved Tom and Buddy out the back door.

Tom approached Joe's clearing with the half-formed intention of telling Miss Chapin's story to Joe and asking him what he knew about the Civil War and the fugitive slaves. Joe was sure to be interested. He might even be one, and if he wasn't, he wouldn't laugh because Tom had got his wars mixed up. However, when Joe greeted him with an especially broad smile and announced that he'd got an extra special treat for the day, Tom forgot about everything else.

"What is it?" He squatted down on the grass beside Joe.

"It's a trip," said Joe, "to the old millpond. There's a spring there, and the water's cool and still, and you can just lay in it all through a hot day. It's a special trip I save for a hot day, and we better start right off before the sun gets any higher." Joe stretched and sat up.

"Is it far?" asked Tom.

"Pretty far. Bring your lunch." Joe got all the way up, removed two eggs from a sauce pan and placed them in a canvas sack. "Hard boiled," he explained. "I've got a little salad." Gently he patted the sack. "It's too hot to cook. We'll drink spring water."

Tom rowed upstream for an hour while Buddy slept and Joe talked to a phoebe. The phoebe kept right along with them and paused frequently in its fly-catching to perch on overhanging branches, pump its tail up and down and repeat its name with variations in a husky whisper. Tom had no breath for whistling. In fact, the longer he rowed, the harder it got, and the less progress he seemed to make. Whenever he paused for a moment to wipe the sweat from his face the boat slipped back downstream.

"Joe," he complained at last, "I'm not getting very far."

Joe made a quick survey of the river and flashed an admiring smile at Tom. "Why," he exclaimed, "You've done fine. You've rowed almost the whole way. We're coming to where the millstream joins in. The current gets real strong. I'll row the rest. It's only justice I should."

They changed seats and, with Joe pulling, made slow but steady progress to the fork and a short distance up the smaller stream. When the stream became too swift to navigate farther, Joe nosed into the bank and shipped his oars.

"She's running full," he said. "We'll have to walk the rest."

They tied the boat, took their lunches, and roused up Buddy, who followed somewhat sullenly as Joe led the way up a slope through scrub oak and juniper and over the crumbling stone walls of abandoned pastures. When a pheasant whirred up from the brush, Buddy cried out in alarm, then stood trembling while with melancholy eyes he implored them to turn back. Joe took him by the collar and helped him over the remaining stone walls. They came out on the stream again just below the mill dam. It was a jumbled pile of mossy stones, clogged with mud and brush, and water spouted or trickled through the chinks.

"The dam's still holding pretty good," remarked Joe as he dragged Buddy up the steep bank.

At the top of the dam lay the pond, half in sun,

half in shadow. At sight of the still, cool water, Buddy lifted his drooping head and plume. He waded in, drank noisily, and with a grunt of contentment sprawled in the water. Two ducks left the pond in alarm and scuttered into the woods on the far side.

"Mallards," said Joe. "They'll be back out of curiosity. Here's the spring."

He threw himself on his stomach and buried his face in a small puddle where water bubbled up between stones and flowed in a tiny stream down to the pond. Joe drank as noisily as Buddy and grunted as contentedly, then he rolled over in the moist grass to make room for Tom to drink.

"Ain't it pretty, and ain't that water sweet?" Joe asked when Tom raised his dripping face from the puddle. "It's worth all the toil of getting to."

Tom drank again, then gazed contentedly over the tips of the grass at the pond. A black and orange butterfly skimmed past his nose, rose jerkily over the pond, and fluttered away into the woods on the far side.

"If I was you," said Tom, still on his stomach in the grass, "I'd camp up here. It's the prettiest, quietest place I've ever seen,"

"Well," Joe was untying his shoe, "I would, except you gotta walk so far and there's no — " he bent over the shoestring, "Well, there ain't so many conveniences."

He finished undressing and submerged himself in

the pond. All through the morning they floated around in the water. It was too hot to really swim. Taking courage from them, Buddy launched himself and churned right across the pond to the far side where he caused the ducks, who were just venturing out on the bank again, to retreat in noisy consternation. Buddy, somewhat taken aback himself, came about and beat his way back to the safer shore. He shook himself, sank down in the shallow water, and didn't budge again.

Joe felt pangs of hunger earlier than usual. "My, I'm hungry," he declared as he sat drying off in the grass. "It must be all that exercise. I wish I'd boiled up three eggs."

From his sack he removed the eggs, a cucumber, a number of tomatoes, and a mess of young lettuce. Carefully, leaf by leaf, he washed the lettuce in the spring.

Tom reached for his own bag of lunch. "Don't worry," he said, "I've got an awful lot of cake." He held up the huge slice and watched Joe's face expand with pleasure.

"Chocolate?" asked Joe.

Tom nodded.

Joe's expression became ecstatic. "Chocolate cake!" He savored the words on his tongue. "I ain't had a piece of real good chocolate cake since I can remember." After a pause, he asked reverently, "Is it real rich chocolate cake?"

Tom nodded again. "And chocolate frosting," he added.

"And you ask why I don't make my camp way up here," cried Joe. "How'd I get real rich chocolate cake with chocolate frosting way up here? How'd I get a friend and a big old dog to keep me company way up here? I'd be lonely and hungry too," said Joe, "which is even worse."

"Were you lonely sometimes before I came?"

Joe pursed his lips judiciously. "You know, I believe I was. Not for crowds. I come here to get away from them, but I believe I was lonely just the same," he smiled at Tom, "because this vacation with you along has been the best yet."

"It's been the best for me too," said Tom. "I'd have been lonely doing things all by myself. With you, though, it's been better than anything."

"Exactly," replied Joe with an understanding nod. He gestured generously at his salad. "Have a tomato. They're nice and fresh. Have some salt on it." He produced a battered cardboard box from his sack. "I carry it with me," he explained. "Just dip in." He peeled an egg, dipped it in salt, and, after a few mouthfuls, he chuckled for pure joy. "If this ain't a real feast. Eggs, salad, and chocolate cake. Have some lettuce, have some cucumber." He overflowed with generosity. He peeled and salted the second egg and bit in. "Yes," he said, "this vacation's had a different feel from the others, and mostly it's been a good feel.

There was bad feels too, like when you first come down with that big dog and said you'd just moved in and why was I painting your boat. That kinda worried me at first. And there was the time when it seemed like they'd got me in the Army again." Joe shook his head.

"Just about everybody was in the Army, I guess," put in Tom conversationally. "My father was and so was — " Tom stopped just in time. He'd been going to say something about Angela's son, Eddy.

"Never mind that." Joe waved the Army aside. "What I'm trying to say is irregardless of some uncomfortable feelings, and notwithstanding, this vacation has been extra special, and it's all because you come to keep me company. I'm proud to share my place, and my boat, and my fish with you. I'm proud to share my learning with you. In short," he gestured with the egg, "if you was hungry now, I'd give you this egg out of my own mouth because you are my friend." Joe drew breath and surveyed the egg with something like surprise. "I wouldn't do that for no one else," he declared as he polished off the egg.

Tom felt his face flushing. "Thanks, Joe," he murmured. "I feel the same way about you, and I'm not a bit hungry now. I'm full." He held the cake toward Joe, but in the excess of his pleasure and embarrassment he couldn't look at him. "You eat it all, Joe. I'm full. Honest I am."

"No sir," Joe slammed one hand down on the grass, "I won't take all your cake. That's not justice. We gotta share. You take a little and give me what's left."

Tom unwrapped the cake, and, as the sunlight glinted on the frosting, Joe gave a low whistle. Tom broke off a small piece for himself and handed the rest to Joe. It completely covered his outstretched hand. Tom nibbled his cake and watched with satisfaction while Joe absorbed his and acquired in the process the familiar expression of pleased and puzzled expectancy. This time, because the piece of cake was so large, Joe was wafted into his after-lunch trance before he'd half finished. With puckered brow and parted lips, he gazed off across the pond. Sometimes he rubbed his head. Sometimes the upturned corners of his mouth twitched into a full smile. Otherwise he was perfectly still.

Tom took another drink from the spring. He threw some crusts on the water to tempt the ducks. They had emerged onto the bank again, and they held a lengthy consultation before the drake, with the brown duck zigzagging at his stern, paddled cautiously out, snatched up the crusts, and beat it back to the shelter of the woods. Still Joe sat entranced. The sun beat down hotter than ever. The pond lay smooth as a mirror. The ducks gave no sign of life. Not a leaf stirred. No birds sang. Like Joe, everything hung torpid in the heat.

131

"How about another swim?" ventured Tom.

"Hush," whispered Joe. He slowly bit into the cake and chewed, but gave no other sign of life.

Tom waded into the pond and lowered himself in the water. He floated luxuriously until he was well cooled, and then set out to swim the circuit of the pond. Swimming slowly toward the old dam which formed an irregular wall of rock sticking up a foot or so above the level of the water, Tom watched for some sign of animal life. Only the ripples gliding off slantwise from his shoulders ruffled the surface of the pond. There was no other stirring anywhere, and perhaps because of the complete stillness, Tom noticed, before he really saw clearly, a faint disturbance on the rocks of the mill dam. Keeping his eyes fixed on the rocks, Tom swam closer and saw something like a snarled fishline lying on them. The fishline seemed to wiggle ever so faintly. Tom trod water and saw what he had taken for a fishline turn, before his eyes, into lots and lots of little black snakes. In a loose tangle, they lay basking on the hot rocks. Except for an occasional flick or squirm, they were motionless as everything else, and it was this tiny bit of movement which had first caught Tom's eye. With his heart pounding, Tom cautiously trod water and studied the snakes. There were at least fifteen of them in the tangle. This was the chance of a lifetime. As silently as he was able Tom swam back to Joe.

132

"The rocks on the dam are covered with snakes," he announced in an agitated whisper.

Joe blinked at him.

"Can I use your sack to put them in?"

Joe blinked again and nodded.

Tom was too excited to wait for Joe. He snatched up the sack, ran around the edge of the pond to the mill dam, and crept on all fours along the rocks. Closer and closer he crawled. The tangle of snakes writhed. Tom grabbed and bagged two snakes. As the snakes darted away among the rocks, Tom grabbed again wildly and got three more. He galloped back to Joe.

"I got some!" He drew a handful of snakes from the sack and waved them at Joe.

Joe started and rubbed his eyes. "Well," he said vaguely.

"Do you know what kind they are?"

It took Joe a long time to focus his eyes on the snakes. "They look like little garter snakes," he said finally. "They make nice pets. Where'd you get 'em?"

"On the dam. I told you. Didn't you see me creep up on them?"

"I guess not." Joe scratched his head. "Maybe I was asleep."

"No, you weren't. You were sitting up, and you said I could use your sack." Tom held out his handful of snakes to admire them. They had two tiny yellow stripes running along their backs. "Aren't they pretty Joe? I lay still in the water and then I crept up along the dam." Joe didn't answer . "What's the matter Joe? I thought you liked snakes."

"I do." Joe rubbed his fists in his eyes. "Only I got a funny feeling."

"You ate too much cake. It's awful rich. It's got a pound of butter in it." Tom sat down, dropped the snakes in the sack and stuck his face in the mouth to watch their squirmings.

"Yes, that's it." Joe spoke eagerly. "It was rich, dark, chocolate cake, and I was sitting at the kitchen table eating it, and the sun was coming in hot through the window, and she was standing there watching me eat, and she said I'd better not eat too much because it was awful rich with a whole pound of butter in it. She turned away and began working around, singing some song."

"Who are you talking about?" Tom came up from the sack.

"Ma," replied Joe. "She made the cake."

Tom sighed. "O.K.," he said soothingly. As Joe continued to stare at nothing, Tom passed the sack to him. "Look at them, Joe. Look how they're sort of all different colors close to. Take one out if you want to and hold him in the light."

Joe pushed the sack aside. "Leave me alone," he said. "I'm trying to remember. It was a slow tune and quiet, like it is here along the river."

Joe had never spoken so sharply to Tom before. His great body was tense. His puzzled expectant look had tightened into a sort of groping frenzy. Hurt and uneasy, Tom watched while Joe clenched his fists and gritted his teeth. Joe heaved a long sigh. He shook his head, and sank back on the grass.

"It's no use," he said.

"What's no use?" Tom asked. Joe looked all worn out.

Joe sighed again. "I try and try, and just when I've almost got it, bang, I'm back in that place, and they're asking me the questions: What's your name? How old are you? Where do you live? Try to think. Take your time. Don't be frightened. Remember! Try to remember! . . . How could I try to think?" Joe raised his head. "How could I remember anything with all them majors and colonels standing around, shooting the questions at me and drilling into me with their eyes? I ask you, how could I?" He turned to Tom who could only shake his head in silent sympathy. "No," continued Joe. "I couldn't. So I run away."

"You run away?"

"They was a big sort of garden round the place, and they was a low wall. I climbed over it," said Joe. "It was easy, but every time I try to remember something nice, I can't. The questions start all over again, and I get to feeling like they was after me again." He glanced over his shoulder. "Even at my own place here by the river." He moved uneasily.

"Joe," Tom leaned toward him, "were you ever a fugitive slave?"

Joe's eyes rolled. "Maybe," he faltered. "I — I don't know. I just got this feeling. I got it bad." He half rose.

"Wait, Joe." Tom touched his knee. "You don't need to be afraid they're after you any more because," now Tom faltered, trying to remember what Elsie had said, "well, because after the war was over they were all free."

"Are you sure of that?"

"Elsie said so, and she's usually right."

Joe scowled thoughtfully. "The war's over all right. I remember that, but I can't remember about being a fugitive slave, not clearly, that is. Tell me some more."

Hesitantly at first, because Joe was so jumpy and unlike himself, and because it was hard to tell about Miss Chapin and her grandmother and make it all clear the way Elsie had, Tom started on his story. Although he tried to remember all the little things, like the doll's house and the summerhouse where the girls had played, and put them in at the right places, Tom kept getting mixed up and having to backtrack. For a while Joe just looked more worried than ever, and Tom wished he'd never brought up the fugitive slaves. However, by the time he got to the part where Althea married and went away, Joe had stopped looking worried. He looked interested. When Tom finished up with the sudden arrival and disappearance of Althea or her ghost, and Joe said, "Well now, that's interesting. I'm glad to know that," in his usual easy way, Tom enjoyed a small private triumph. Elsie wasn't the only one who could tell a story so it made you forget everything else.

"You know," said Joe reflectively, "I don't believe I'm one of them old fugitive slaves. They was too long ago."

"That's what I wasn't sure of," said Tom.

"I'm sure," said Joe, "but I'm glad to know about them. It makes me feel like my little place by the river is a real home because there's been others like me there before. You know what it is?" Joe grinned. "It's my ancestral estate."

"Yes," replied Tom, "I guess so, in a way, only what about Althea?"

"Don't you worry about her," said Joe. "Her troubles was over long ago. And Tom, there's no ghosts in that house."

"That's what Angela says, but — " Tom bit his tongue. He hadn't meant to bring up Angela, especially now, when Joe was just feeling comfortable again.

Joe didn't seem as annoyed as usual. "She's right," he said. "There's no such things, and you shouldn't worry."

"I don't," said Tom. "I just go to sleep, but the

noise wakes Elsie up, and she's afraid it's a ghost."

"What noise is that?"

"It's a kind of a squeak and a thump. I only heard it the first night, but Elsie hears it much oftener. She wakes up and cries."

"The poor little thing!" exclaimed Joe. "I'd never have thought — "

"I know," put in Tom, "she's an awful baby in some ways, even though she's so old. Everyone knows it's just the pump or the furnace or maybe a door banging, but she has to get all worked up."

"The poor little thing!" Joe shook his head over and over.

"You don't need to feel sorry for her," Tom reassured him. "Angela always gets up and comforts her, and my father is spending lots of money getting the pump fixed and the furnace fixed, and today Angela's oiling all the doors."

Angela had slipped in again. Tom glanced quickly at Joe to see how he was taking it. He was taking it well.

"Now that's a smart idea," he nodded, "a real smart idea. I wouldn't want the little thing to be frightened."

"Aw, she's all right." Tom turned his attention back to the snakes. "Look at them, Joe. You think I can tame them?"

Joe pulled out a snake, examined it closely, and nodding in a knowledgeable way, he said, "These here little garter snakes make real nice pets. You build 'em a nice cage with some water in it, and you keep 'em near you and catch flies for 'em, and they'll be real friendly and affectionate. I'd take one myself if I didn't move around so much."

"Take one," said Tom. "You don't move around much."

Joe shook his head. "I travel. It's no life even for a snake." He replaced the snake in the sack.

"Where do you travel?"

"All over," Joe stretched. "But of all the places I been, I like it here along the river best."

"Then why don't you always just stay here? I wish you would."

"The winters here," said Joe seriously, "gets too cold and damp. It ain't comfortable."

Winter on this heat-laden afternoon was hard to imagine, and yet, Tom sighed, school and winter without Joe lay somewhere ahead. He sighed again, and Joe seemed to understand his thoughts.

"I'm not thinking about winter now," he said, "and don't you neither. With this nice sun ripenin' the corn, and us fishin' and eatin' together, and no worries to speak of except when I bring 'em on by working too hard with my brain," Joe tapped his forehead, "why should we think about winter which is a long way off? I feel like it's time for a cool drink and another swim. This day's a real scorcher."

Lying on his back in the middle of the pond, Joe

quacked at the ducks. They had ventured out again on the bank, and Joe's remarks threw them into a dither which verged on hysteria. Swayed alternately by curiosity and timidity, they flustered between the bank and the water, demanding explanations of Joe, imploring each other to be careful, and collapsing at intervals into the duck equivalent of hysterical laughter. Tom was so overcome with giggles that he had to rest with Buddy in the shallow water. He couldn't keep himself afloat.

In midafternoon, with Buddy and the sack of snakes, they slipped downstream to Joe's camp. There Tom lay down in the shade, for in such heat even the slight effort of sitting upright and guiding the boat was exhausting. Joe, however, was restless.

"Gotta do an errand," he muttered as he fumbled around in his duffel bag.

"Supper?" inquired Tom. "Gee, I wouldn't think you'd be hungry again so soon."

"Gotta go to town. It's a long walk. Gotta start early to get there before the stores close." Joe felt deep inside the duffel bag and came up with a wallet. He opened it, and, after a long inspection of its contents, he nodded and stuffed it in his pocket. "Isn't it about time?" He looked hard at Tom.

"Yeah," Tom got up, "I guess so, only you're starting much earlier than usual."

"I got an important errand in town," said Joe. "You can keep my sack till you get a cage for the snakes. I won't be needin' it tonight because I got another, but with this hot sun ripenin' the corn, in a day or so, I'll be needin' both sacks." For a few minutes Joe surveyed the torrid western sky. "Hope the weather holds," he muttered. He turned and picked up his empty sack. "Gotta hustle." He flapped his hand at Tom. "See you tomorrow."

Tom whistled up Buddy and started for home with the snakes.

CHAPTER 12

Tom climbed the slope to the house considering in his mind what he should use to make a suitable cage for the snakes. He would need a strong wooden box and some screening, and he ought to start work right away. Joe wanted the sack back in a day or so, and Angela was sure to take a dim view of snakes loose in the house. Just before he came up to the clothesyard and the twins, Tom turned abruptly and went around to the front of the house. If the twins didn't see him now, he would have time to work on the cage before racing time, and if Angela didn't know about the snakes until they were safely caged, so much the better. He approached the front door so engrossed in plans for the cage that he gave only a passing glance to the Cadillac parked in the driveway. He pushed open the big front door, which swung soundlessly on its oiled hinges. With his foot on the threshold he stopped and jerked the bag of snakes behind his back. In the hall, close against the half-opened parlor door, and with one ear thrust well into the opening, stood Angela. From the parlor Tom heard the voices of his mother and father, subdued, almost muffled, and another unknown woman's voice, not at all subdued.

"George is nobody's fool, let me tell you. He's right on his toes, and he has both feet on the ground too. That's how he makes his money." The unknown voice brayed out through the hall. A faint tinkling as of a spoon on glass followed. "This iced tea is really very good. I don't mind if I do have some more." The bray subsided to a penetrating cackle. "Aren't you lucky to have a servant these days. Most of us find them so unreasonable that we'd rather get along without and do our own work, not that we can't afford to pay the wages, you understand." The words stopped, but the cackle swelled into a bleat of self-satisfaction.

Trembling ever so slightly, Angela pressed her ear farther into the opening of the door. With great care Tom stepped into the hall. If he could just slip past Angela and get upstairs with the snakes, all would be well. He took a second careful step and a third. A floor board groaned. Angela didn't jump guiltily as people caught eavesdropping are supposed to do. She turned slowly. Tom had plenty of time to face around and keep the snakes out of sight, but Angela's eyes, as he first saw them turning on him, glowed with such ferocity that his heart skipped a beat. Her eyes softened as they rested on Tom. She put a finger to her lips, jerked her head toward the parlor door, and beckoning Tom to follow, tiptoed down the hall toward the kitchen. Tom had no choice. With the snakes tucked up against his backbone he tiptoed after her. Angela carefully shut the kitchen door. She raised both arms, lifted her face to the ceiling and drew a deep breath.

"Oh Lord," she boomed, "if You could see fit to loose a bolt of lightning, a flood, or a pestilence and destroy that woman and her husband and all their worldly goods, but spare the child, Lord, for he knows not what he does, if, Lord, You could destroy them (and spare the child), we, Your meek and humble servants would sing Your praises, Lord, and we would be able to love one another as You want us to. Only these serpents that have come amongst us, them we cannot love, Oh Lord, we cannot."

At the mention of serpents Tom's heart skipped another beat. Angela often spoke to the Lord, but her hitting on the serpents was uncanny. Tom stood at uneasy attention while Angela sank down on a kitchen chair and wiped her brow.

"Forgive me, Lord," she sighed. "It's partly the heat. Thy will be done."

With the snakes squirming against his back Tom waited for Angela to give her orders. She just sat there frowning and biting her lip.

"What serpents?" Tom ventured timidly.

"Creels," exploded Angela. "Mean, creeping, poison-fanged Creels!"

144

"Creels?" Tom's eyes widened.

"Yes, Creels," cried Angela, "and you'd better know about them now so that when you grow up you'll be on your guard and you won't be bitten like your poor foolish daddy."

"I've got to go upstairs," Tom sidled backward.

"No." Angela raised her great hand. Tom stood still. "You shall hear," declared Angela. "Mr. Creel is the real estate man who owned this house and sold it to your poor daddy." Tom tried to look bright. "He distinctly told your daddy that the land on the north side reached just about to the stone wall and that all the land beyond was part of a large estate with the house down by the river. Like all scoundrels," Angela's bosom heaved, "Mr. Creel wasn't exactly lying, but he wasn't telling the truth either, not he, oh, the evil creeping serpent!" Angela clenched her teeth and contained her wrath. "Your daddy's land doesn't go within ten feet of that stone wall, and the large estate belongs to Mr. Creel himself, and he's going to build a row of houses right up next to us, right where I'd planned to grow my vegetables. The bulldozers are coming tomorrow to drive a road down to the river."

"Not all the way down to the river?" Tom cried out in alarm.

"Oh, yes," Angela rose up and paced the floor, "and it all wouldn't be so bad if that female serpent, that Mrs. Creel, hadn't come, pretending to make a friendly call, when all the time she couldn't wait to tell your poor mother and daddy how her husband had made fools of them, how he'd been going to have this house torn down when they came along and bought it for twice the price he'd expected to get. 'Of course,'" Angela's lip curled, and she went on with all the self-satisfied barnyard cadences of the visitor in the parlor, " 'no nice people would have bought George's new houses with this old wreck standing right next door, and even though the homes George will put up aren't at all what we'd care to live in ourselves, still George wants to sell to good reliable people, and where we are, by the river, we won't have to have anything to do with them. It wasn't until this old place had been bought and painted up so that at least it was respectable that George felt he could go ahead. George has real business sense.'" Angela broke into a hideous imitation of the bleating laugh, then she gripped a chair and shook it. "Your mother," she cried in her own ringing contralto, "who is always polite and kind, had made that — that snake welcome, and her skinny little boy too. She gave him a cooky and took him by the hand and led him upstairs to see Elsie so he wouldn't be bored sitting with the grownups, and I, fool that I am, made iced tea and cucumber sandwiches with my own hands and served them to that reptile in the parlor as if she was a lady." Angela glared at her huge fists. "When I walked in with the

146

tray, she looked at me as if I was some kind of monster. 'Oh,' she says to your mother, 'I didn't know you had a servant. I suppose she's some help with the housework, but I'd be afraid to have anyone so big and black around my house. Do you dare trust her with the children?' Your mother blushed for the woman. She said, 'Mrs. Gittens is the most trustworthy person I know. She is our friend.' Then your poor daddy came in all unsuspecting and ready to be polite and enjoy his tea and sandwiches." Angela gave the chair a final shake. "I heard the rest through the door." She threw back her head. "If there is anything which can be done to thwart those serpents, Oh Lord, which You in Your Majesty cannot stoop to do, You have only to whisper it to me, and it shall be done." With head thrown back and arms outstretched, Angela stood waiting.

A whistle filled the room. Angela sighed and marched to the speaking tube. She opened the cover.

"Yes?" she said into the mouthpiece.

"Angela!" Elsie's voice shrilled out. "How long do I have to put up with this Creel child? He's driving me crazy, and Paddy too, and in her condition it's very bad for her. When's he going home?"

"Soon," replied Angela. "Tell him to come down to his mother. She can look after him."

"I already have, and he won't." Elsie's voice shook. "He says he always does the opposite of what people tell him to. I can't manage him, Angela, I

147

simply can't, and I don't see why I'm always the one — "

Angela frowned. "You come on down then and bring in the twins. Tell him not to come with you and maybe he will."

"Well, I'll try, but honestly you've no idea what he's like."

Angela let the cover snap to. "What can you expect with parents like his?" she demanded of Tom.

Tom had had plenty of time to realize the enormity of what Mr. Creel proposed to do. "They've got no right to build a road right down to the river," he shouted. "It doesn't belong to them. They've got no right to spoil everything." In his fury, he started to put up his fists, then he remembered the snakes and with his hands clenched awkwardly behind him, plunged backwards toward the stairs.

"Careful," admonished Angela, "and don't you pick any fights with that boy. We've got enough trouble as it is. Vengeance belongs to the Lord." She cast a swift, reminding glance upward. "Run the twins' bath," she said to Tom. "Lukewarm. I'll start their supper." She turned away.

On the stairs Tom encountered Elsie, who shot him a single meaningful glance and clattered on down. In his own room Tom discovered the boy, no more than seven or eight and, as Angela had said, skinny. He was fiddling with the cover to the speaking tube. He gave Tom a long looking over, and apparently not at all impressed by what he saw, he returned his attention to the speaking tube. Tom dropped the bag of snakes in a corner and addressed the boy in what he hoped was a manly and condescending tone.

"You're supposed to go downstairs to your mother."

"Why?" asked the boy.

"Because you are," returned Tom, "and anyway this is my room."

The boy gave Tom another long look. Although he was a good head shorter, he managed to seem to be looking down.

"I got a better room than this," he said, and, wandering over to Tom's playbox, he coolly took stock of its contents. "I've got better toys too. I got an electric train, and an Erector set, and a television." He returned to the speaking tube and snapped it some more.

"Leave that alone. You'll break it." Tom's voice came out shrill and not at all manly.

"I'm not hurting it," replied the boy. He stood on tiptoe and put his eye to the hole. "What would happen if I dropped something in. Would it come out?"

"Yes. Now go on down to your mother. She wants you."

"Let her wait," said the boy.

Tom's face flushed with annoyance. "You get out

149

of my room. I got to do something, and I don't want you around bothering me." Tom glanced hastily at the bag of snakes, and realizing that the boy had noticed his glance, he clenched his fists and glared at the boy.

"You can't make me," said the boy.

With threatening fists, and a hideous frown on his forehead, Tom sidled up to the boy in the menacing manner of a prizefighter.

The boy gave a confident chuckle. "You can't hit me," he said, "because I'm smaller and if you do, I'll throw up. That's what I always do. I did it at camp. I was at camp all summer. I bet you weren't."

"What's so wonderful about that?" yelled Tom. "Who cares where you were? This is my room. You gotta get out. You — you — " He choked and shook with rage.

The boy eyed him coolly. "I don't want to," he said.

Tom clenched his teeth and controlled his shaking. He wiped his forehead. He drew several deep unrefreshing breaths. The heat seemed suddenly to be stifling. He spoke very slowly to hide the fact that he was panting.

"Your mother doesn't want you. You can stay here forever. I don't mind. You stay right here. Don't go away."

"You can't fool me that way," said the boy with another confident chuckle, "I'm bright."

"Tom," Elsie called up the stairs, "hurry up. You haven't even started their bath, and I'm not going to stand here holding both of them all night."

With a strong feeling of relief, Tom hurried to the door. Some remnants of pride and a strong sense of righteous indignation made him turn on the threshold to growl at the boy. "Don't you touch anything in this room. Understand?"

The boy was snapping at the speaking tube again. He gave no sign of having heard.

"I'm telling you," warned Tom.

The boy went right on snapping. Tom retreated downstairs.

"Gee," murmured Tom as he relieved Elsie of Richard. "That kid upstairs ought to be locked up."

"What he needs," replied Elsie, "is a good flogging." She plopped Paul into the tub.

The twins were well trained by now, and, like true thoroughbreds, they raced with all their hearts. They galloped magnificently through cereal and eggs, then Richard, who had won the first two heats by a nose, choked on the home stretch to lose the bottle and his chance for a clean sweep. Tom couldn't be angry with a loser who had tried so hard. While Elsie scolded Paul for slacking, Tom patted his own entry on the back and whispered encouragement in his ear. The excitement of the race temporarily drove the infamous Creels from Tom's mind. However, as soon as he and Elsie descended to the kitchen to leave the supper dishes, the Creels reasserted themselves with a vengeance.

"Digby dear, Mother is calling. Come at once, Digby. Come to Mother. Mother is going home." Mrs. Creel called from the front hall in a genteel whinny.

There was no response.

"Digby, come to Mother. Come at once. Mother is in a hurry. Digby!" This time the whinny was more agitated, less genteel.

"Digby! You hear me. You know you do. You come here!" All trace of gentility was gone. The whinny had risen to a scream.

Still no reply. Footsteps pounded toward the kitchen. Mrs. Creel burst in the door.

"Where's Digby?" she shouted. Her bosom heaved. Beads of sweat stood out on her heavily powdered nose and forehead.

Angela's eyes narrowed. "In my kitchen," she replied, "people say please."

Mrs. Creel gave an indignant grunt. Angela, enormous and exuding hostility, stood her ground and glared. Mrs. Creel fell back a step. With a forced smile she turned to Tom and Elsie.

"Do you know where Digby is?"

"He was upstairs," said Tom.

"Get him for me," whinnied Mrs. Creel, "like a good boy." She simpered.

"He won't come for me," said Tom, "but maybe

he will if you call him through the speaking tube."

"Speaking tube?" Mrs. Creel snorted. She eyed Tom with suspicion. "Don't try to be smart with me. I'm in a hurry."

"It's over there." Tom pointed "First you blow, then you open it and stick your ear against it and wait for him to answer."

Mrs. Creel bridled and emitted an indignant bleat. "I don't like fresh little boys. I won't touch it. I never heard of such a thing."

"You should have," said Elsie. "They were in common use in the old days."

Mrs. Creel's face reddened. Her eyes swept the three faces confronting her. Tom and Elsie regarded her with round, innocent eyes. Angela's lips twitched.

Beside herself, Mrs. Creel opened her mouth and screamed, "Digby, you come here!"

The echoes died. Silence followed.

"You better try the speaking tube," advised Tom.

Muttering a string of highly ungenteel words, Mrs. Creel approached the speaking tube. She blew, opened the cover, and put her ear to the hole.

A little black snake poked out his head, slithered onto Mrs. Creel's shoulder, and dove down her neck. A second little snake followed. Mrs. Creel's screams as she staggered back far surpassed all her previous demonstrations. She clutched at her clothing and breaking into a gallop began to circle the kitchen.

153

The third little snake had been caught midway as the cover snapped shut. Its forward half writhed miserably in the air. With a cry of alarm Tom jumped to its rescue and held the cover open so that the fourth and fifth could come out too. The fourth came right along and he caught it, but the fifth was slow. Tom waited at the tube, and, as Mrs. Creel continued to buck and prance around the kitchen, he felt growing concern for the snakes she was carrying with her.

"Look out," he cried. "Please look out. You'll hurt them."

His eyes darted from the tube to Mrs. Creel who had begun to spin like a top. "Hurry," he cried into the tube, but the snake didn't come. Still spinning, Mrs. Creel tore viciously at her skirt and stamped her feet. In desperation Tom turned to Elsie.

"Please catch the snakes when she shakes them loose. Please, Elsie. She's going to stamp on them and kill them."

Elsie didn't hear him. She was staring entranced at Mrs. Creel.

"There's only four," said a voice in Tom's ear. "The other one got away. It went in your sister's room. I've been looking for it, but I can't find it."

At this moment Mrs. Creel shook out her snakes. Tom gave a frantic cry, but Digby, quick as lightning, darted in and snatched the snakes from under his mother's stamping feet.

"I bet you couldn't do that," he said as he handed the snakes to the astonished Tom.

Mrs. Creel stood still, panting. Her clothes were disheveled. Her painted face was streaked and smudged. Digby surveyed her with a cool, discerning eye.

"Boy," he said, "if you could see yourself — "

Mrs. Creel lunged and caught him by the arm. Gasping for breath, she dragged him to the door. Digby hung back and grinned at Tom.

"I bet you wish you'd thought of that." As he disappeared through the door he waved his free arm. "I told you I was bright," he said.

It took Tom a long time to make clear to his family that Digby, not he, had put the snakes in the speaking tube. Mr. and Mrs. Stackpole were too depressed to take pleasure in the discomfiture of Mrs. Creel, but Angela interpreted the incident as a hopeful sign.

"The Lord is watching over us," she declared as she set about cooking dinner.

Tom put together a temporary cage for the four snakes he had left, then he crawled all over the third floor looking for the one that had got away. Like his parents, he felt too unhappy about the housing development to take much interest or pleasure in anything. His thoughts, as he crawled around, turned constantly to Joe. Now Joe would be cooking supper at his place, lying under the trees, whistling to the birds. Tomorrow the bulldozers would knock down

Joe's trees and drive Joe from the place he liked best in the whole world, and Joe would be gone forever. A sob rose in Tom's throat. Tears sprang to his eyes, and the floor boards wavered and blurred. Tom gave up hunting. He sat on the floor wondering how he could get through the rest of his life if Joe was gone forever.

Dinner was a dismal affair.

"Richard, you must see your lawyer. Surely there is something he can do to stop Mr. Creel from building right on top of us."

"I'll see him," replied Mr. Stackpole, "though I don't know that it will be any use."

Elsie tossed her pigtails. "If necessary," she said, "we can always buy him off."

"We could," said Mr. Stackpole, "if we had any money to buy him with."

"Don't you have any money?" Elsie turned anxiously to her father.

Mr. Stackpole laughed bitterly. "The house has eaten it all up, Elsie. Your Miss Chapin is right. First it was Follonsbee. Now it's Stackpole. Stackpole's Folly." He groaned.

"Oh Daddy!" Elsie wilted. Tears came to her eyes.

"Mr. Stackpole," Angela stepped to his side, "I have $5000 I don't need. It's what I saved for Eddy to go to college. I don't need it any more. You see if your lawyer can't make a deal to buy that land up to the stone wall. It ought to be enough for that."

"No, Angela, I can't do it. I can't take your money."

"Of course you can." Angela laid her hand reassuringly on Mr. Stackpole's shoulder. "I've been wondering what to do with that money, and now I know. I've come to like this house, and I like the country around it. We all like it, and I'm going to have a vegetable garden."

"No, no." Mr. Stackpole shook his head.

Angela tightened her grip on his shoulder. "You can't refuse, Mr. Stackpole. The Lord wants you to have that money."

"Angela," put in Mrs. Stackpole, "we are very grateful, but we can't take your savings. They are yours. You must use them for yourself."

"There's no other way I could use them that would give me so much pleasure," returned Angela. "Come, Mr. Stackpole," she shook him gently as if he were a small boy, "don't give up. You see your lawyer first thing tomorrow, and you just let him manage it. Your lawyer's a business man. With $5000 to work with he ought to be able to find some way of keeping that Creel out of my vegetable garden." She gave Mr. Stackpole a final encouraging shake and let him go.

"I hope you're right, Angela," said Mr. Stackpole meekly.

"I usually am," replied Angela.

She cast her eye over the untasted food and the dejected forms around the table.

"It's too hot to eat," she said. "We will all sing hymns. You too, Mr. Stackpole. You'll be surprised how it cheers you up."

With Angela's voice booming above the rest, they sang in unison all her favorite hymns from "The Son of God Goes Forth to War" to "By Cool Siloam's Shady Rill." The sweat poured down their faces. Mrs. Stackpole's fingers stuck to the piano keys, but the singing did have a cheering or at least a quieting effect. In spite of the heat which lingered on through the night, everyone slept soundly, undisturbed either by ghostly sounds from the past or dismal premonitions of the future.

CHAPTER 13

THE SUN next morning filtered sickly
yellow through haze, but the heat clung thicker and
heavier even than on the day before. Mr. Stackpole
set off early to see his lawyer in town.

"Take your raincoat," said Angela. "It feels like
a storm."

To Tom as he set off with his packet of lunch she
said, "Don't go far off. There's going to be a storm."

For the first time in his life Buddy refused to come
to Tom's repeated commands and whistles. He curled
up in a corner of the kitchen and pretended to be
both deaf and paralyzed.

Before going to the river Tom walked all around
the field looking for bulldozers. He was relieved not
to find any, and he tried hard to persuade himself that
no bulldozers was a good omen and that everything
was going to be all right. However, as he made his
way over the familiar ground toward Joe's camp, he
felt a strangeness about him. The blackberry vines as
he broke through them were limp and strangely
drained of color. In the woods, the well-known

rustlings and hummings had a subdued and furtive quality. The river itself looked oily and unfamiliar. When, from far off, he caught the rumble of thunder, he felt with a certainty which defied reason that all these portents of an approaching storm were also portents of approaching evil, and that they far outweighed his one good omen.

Joe lolled as usual by the ashes of his cooking fire. "Storm coming," he said. "Gotta expect something bad after all this fine weather." He sat up and began in his usual luxurious manner to scratch his back.

The sight of Joe, all at ease and unsuspecting, smote Tom like a blow, and his words "Gotta expect something bad" rang like another evil portent in Tom's ears. The wood was terribly still. Tom strained his ears for some little familiar chirp or rustle to muffle the ominous reverberations of Joe's words.

"Sleep well?" asked Joe. Tom nodded absently.

"Guess there weren't no ghost noises last night," Joe said comfortably. When Tom, listening still to the hushed woods, didn't reply, Joe tapped his leg. "Your sister didn't hear no ghost noises last night, did she?"

"No," said Tom and sat down on the grass. He couldn't put his mind on Joe's conversation. He couldn't stop listening, dreading another bad omen and at the same time hoping, praying almost, to hear something reassuring, something good.

Joe gave a little laugh. "That was a smart idea of

161

hers," he said, "oiling the hinges."

"What?" Tom tried to wrench his mind from listening.

"I said that was a good idea of hers to oil the hinges."

"That wasn't Elsie's idea," said Tom, and then his back stiffened. He heard a strange sound in the silent woods.

"I know that," said Joe. "It was the other one."

Tom sat rigid.

"What's her name?" asked Joe.

Tom heard the sound again, a stirring in the woods behind him, and then it was lost in another rumble of thunder.

"Tom, I asked you a question. What's the name of the one that oiled the hinges?"

Was it a squirrel, thought Tom, or a mouse, and was it good or bad?

"Tom, are you deaf? What's the name of the one that oiled the hinges?"

"Oh, Angela," muttered Tom. Again he heard the sound, stealthy, it seemed, and creeping, not reassuring. His fingernails dug into the ground. Sweat broke out on his forehead.

"I mean her second name, Tom. She must have a second name."

"Gittens," said Tom impatiently, and he quickly turned on the sound certain that he'd see Mr. Creel or a bulldozer leering at him from the bushes. The

162

trees and bushes were completely still. Their leaves hung motionless, an intense and livid green. There was no sign of Mr. Creel or his bulldozers. The thunder rumbled again.

It's just the storm, Tom told himself, and turning from the woods he looked up at the sky.

Above him it was hazy yellow, but to the west leaden thunderheads were gathering.

"Gittens," Joe repeated softly, "Gittens."

Tom made a determined effort to shake off his forebodings. It's the storm, he said over and over to himself. The thunder rumbled again, and in the hush that followed Tom heard the rustling sound again. Wind, he told himself, wind, but he knew it wasn't wind. There wasn't so much as a breath. Tom could bear his forebodings no longer. He felt he must tell Joe. Joe might as well know the worst.

"Joe." He turned sadly to his friend.

Joe held up a warning hand. Although he'd finished breakfast some time ago, his face wore that wrapt expression which usually came on only at the end of a meal.

"I gotta tell you something, Joe," Tom spoke hurriedly to catch Joe before he went into his complete trance.

"Hush," said Joe, and to Tom's amazement, he burst into the hymn "By Cool Siloam's Shady Rill." His voice rang deep and true. Swaying slightly, he rolled confidently through all three verses. As his

163

voice died away, the thunder muttered like an echo, then silence closed in. Tom gazed open-mouthed at Joe, while Joe, with lips curved in a half smile, stared straight ahead at nothing. A twig snapped in the woods behind them. Both spun round. There was nothing to be seen.

Joe's face contorted. "I gotta stop trying," he cried. "I'm back to where they're after me again." He glanced around like a hunted animal. "Tom!" His fist closed on Tom's arm, "We gotta do something so I'll stop trying before they're after me again and it's too late. I gotta forget." He pulled Tom to his feet. "We'll take a swim." He dragged Tom to the river, tore off his clothes, and dived in.

Tom hesitated on the bank. The thunder clouds had crowded higher up the sky. They cast their leaden shadow on the river. Joe's words "Before it's too late" pounded in Tom's head. To escape them he dived. The cool, sweet-smelling water closed over him. The current tugged with soft sure fingers. He came to the surface, and like a bird or a fish he swooshed off downstream. A flash of lightning knifed through the clouds in the west. The thunder rumbled. A wild exhilaration seized Tom. If Joe hadn't yelled at him, he'd have forgotten to strike for shore in time. He beat his way into the still water and squatted beside Joe in the shallows.

"What a sensation," sighed Joe. "I knew it'd make me feel better."

Tom leaned back in the water and watched the lightning leap about the sky. The thunder clouds were hanging right overhead. A tingling excitement filled the air. Suddenly Tom realized that he felt better too. The heavy foreboding was gone. He kicked his legs in the water and laughed in relief.

"Swimming's great exercise," remarked Joe, "and it stirs up an appetite."

"What do you want to eat now?" Tom laughed.

Joe sucked his cheeks reflectively. "A piece of that chocolate cake would be real nice," he murmured, "but I don't suppose you'd have any today."

"Maybe there is," Tom jumped to his feet. "I'll see. I'll bring it down here. We can eat it sitting by the water. We'll just have time before the storm."

Tom raced along the bank and turned up the path to Joe's clearing. He felt cool and light and full of hope. Then he caught his breath and stopped in his tracks. There in the grass with his mouth stretched wide to receive the piece of chocolate cake he was in the act of stuffing into it squatted Digby. For a minute Tom could neither move nor speak. He saw Digby's teeth closing on the cake.

"Hey," he screamed and sprang at Digby.

Digby dropped the cake. He jumped straight into the air and cut back for the woods. With a roar Tom headed him off. Quick as lightning Digby slipped from Tom's outstretched arms and darted off up-stream. Tom crashed through the brush and again

165

managed to head him off. Now he had him at bay. With his back to the river, Digby faced Tom. Making futile little dashes to one side and the other as Tom bore down, Digby was forced back step by step toward the river. Tom swelled with a sense of power and righteous wrath.

"You're a spy and a thief," growled Tom. Relentlessly he closed in.

"I'm a scout," quavered Digby. "I was scouting." His eyes shifted craftily from side to side.

The thunder boomed close by. A breath of wind set the grass and leaves aquiver. Digby, as he dodged backward, quivered too.

"Wait till I get my hands on you," threatened Tom.

"You can't hit me," shrilled Digby, "because if you do, I'll throw up," and he made a sudden dash for escape which was so nearly successful that it left Tom panting, shaking, and choked with rage.

He clenched his fists. "I'll, I'll — " and he drove Digby to the edge of the river.

"What's got into you, Tom? Why're you chasing that little boy?"

The boom of Joe's voice, like a boom of thunder, and the sudden appearance of Joe himself, enormous, black, and glistening wet, were too much for Digby's nervous system. With a shriek he turned his back on Tom and threw himself into the river.

"Hey, you little boy," called Joe, "you come back.

166

Don't you get in that current." Joe ran up the bank. "Tom," he scolded, "what's the matter with you?"

Digby paddled in distracted circles in the slack water.

"Come back in," ordered Joe. "Come right back in."

Digby headed straight out. The current snatched him. Joe dived in after.

Shaking worse than ever, as a gust of cold wind swept across the water, Tom watched in horror as Joe struck out after Digby. Another stronger gust ripped the surface of the river, and seemed, as well as Tom could tell, for the light was dim and the lightning flickered wildly, to sweep the two bobbing heads faster and faster downstream. Joe's arms flashed up and down. He was gaining. He was on top of Digby, and then, whisked aside by some trick of the current, Digby spun out of reach, and again Joe was beating after him. Tom looked wildly around. He must help Joe. The boat was tied to a tree just at hand. Tom ran to untie it. His shaking fingers tugged and pulled at the knot, and the knot held fast. He glanced downstream. The heads were together now, two darker specks in a murky twilight which combined air and water. Lightning flashed. Joe had Digby, but they were beyond the tree. They were whizzing straight on downstream. Tom dropped the rope, grabbed up an oar, and raced with it down the bank. Another gust, chill as death, chased him as he tore out on the spit and splashed into the shallow water at its end. Tom stretched his oar out across the water. He was only just in time. Joe, with Digby under one arm, swept past, and managed with his free hand to grab the oar and hang on. Tom dug his heels in and pulled. The oar with Joe clinging to it swung in an arc around Tom. His feet slipped. His arms were nearly torn from their sockets, but he held on until Joe was swung around into the shallow water. With heaving chest and Digby squirming under his arm Joe waded in.

"That was fine, Tom," panted Joe. "I was hoping you'd think to do that."

Joe set Digby down on his feet and held his shoulders to steady him. Digby swayed for a minute and wiped the water from his face, then he turned a delighted smile on Joe.

"Boy," he said, "did you see me swim? Boy, I guess I'm the best swimmer you ever saw. I am the best swimmer you ever saw, aren't I? Swish! Swoosh! Aren't I fast? Let's do it again. This time I bet you can't catch me."

Joe's mouth fell open. He was still panting, and for a moment he couldn't speak.

"Come on," urged Digby. "I bet this time I'll win."

"Little boy," Joe laid a trembling hand on his shoulder, "little boy," he shook his head and his face creased up, "you and I was almost drownded. If Tom

168

hadn't come up with the oar, we'd be over the falls by now, if we hadn't smashed against the bridge first, or just plain sunk to the bottom. Tom here saved our lives."

Tom sputtered. "I didn't save his life. I tried to save yours, but not his."

"Tom," Joe turned in consternation, "what's got into you today? Ain't you got no milk of human kindness?"

"Listen, Joe," Tom's teeth were chattering, "you d-don't know h-him. H-he w-was eating your c-cake."

A flash of lightning ripped open the sky. The crash which followed shook the earth.

"We gotta get to shelter," said Joe. "Where do you live?" he asked Digby.

"Right there," said Digby pointing upstream, "but I don't want to go home. I want — "

The thunder exploded again right on top of them, and a wind, not a gust but a driving gale, bent all the trees before it and held them tossing feebly and unable to straighten. Again the thunder crashed. Digby didn't finish his sentence. He whizzed up the bank and disappeared in the bushes. While thunder cracked and lightning ripped and the wind swept over them, Tom and Joe hastily pulled on their clothes.

"You run home quick. Rain's coming." Joe was gathering up his belongings and stuffing them in the duffel bag.

Tom started, but ran back to Joe. "Where can you go to keep dry?"

Joe was still picking up. "I'm all right," he said, "I got a place." The thunder burst again, and with a long sigh, all the trees and shrubs bent double before the wind.

"Where?" Tom shouted. He tugged at Joe's sleeve. "I don't see any place. You'll get soaked."

"Never mind where," Joe shouted back. "I tell you I'm all right. If you want to do me a favor though, you just leave me your sandwiches. Did that boy eat all the cake? Because if he didn't — " Joe's voice was lost in a thunderclap.

"There," Tom pointed, "he dropped it there." A raindrop splattered on his neck.

"Get along," shouted Joe.

With the wind pushing from behind and the raindrops spanging against his back, Tom raced out of the wood, up the hill, and burst in the kitchen door just as the deluge broke. Angela was waiting, ready, he could tell, to scold him, but the sudden impact of the rain stopped her. It burst over the house with a sound like the rolling of drums. Thunder, lightning, and wind were extinguished in the flood which roared from the sky. Tom and Angela stood at the kitchen window staring amazed into what looked like a solid wall of water.

"The bulldozers can't work today anyway, can they, Angela?" Tom asked hopefully as the first deluge let up slightly and gave him a glimpse of the empty sodden field.

"No," replied Angela. "The Lord must have heard me." The rain closed down again. "I didn't mean Him to go too far though." She looked uneasily at the ceiling. "You should have come home sooner." She pounced on Tom. "I was worried about you all alone down there with the storm coming on. I had a caller this morning." Angela squared her shoulders and tossed her head. "He came here especially to call on me, and in the course of our conversation he told me that that river has a strong current. You should be careful down there. He said something else too. He said that people living along the river had been losing vegetables from their gardens. Tom Stackpole," Angela shook her finger at him, "I hope you can look me in the eye and say you don't know anything about that."

"I don't, Angela, honest." Tom looked Angela straight in the eye, and his thoughts slid quite naturally from vegetables to Joe who often spoke about them especially in the evening when he was planning his supper. He had two sacks for carrying vegetables. Tom suddenly dropped his eyes. He felt his face flushing.

"I'm glad to hear it," replied Angela. "I told my caller I didn't believe you'd ever do a thing like that unless you were led astray by bad companions."

Tom, staring hard at his feet, was grateful for the

171

dim light and drumming rain. Oh Joe, he thought, poor Joe.

"You're a good boy by nature," Angela went on in a lecturing way, "but you're easily led astray." She cleared her throat. "As I told my visitor," she continued, "and he agreed with me ('You're absolutely right, Mrs. Gittens,' he said, 'absolutely right'), boys should be raised in the country where there's room for them to fan around. In the city," Angela's voice boomed above the noise of the rain, "boys are crowded together too much, and the goats lead the sheep into ways of evil, and the sheep, being what they are, follow." Angela heaved a mighty sigh. "Eddy was a sheep, and you are a sheep, and don't you go picking up any strangers and making friends with them until I've looked them over and passed on them. They might be goats." She wagged her finger under Tom's nose.

Tom swallowed. "Who was your visitor?" he asked timidly. He strongly suspected that he was a member of the police force.

"My visitor," replied Angela with a toss of the head, "was the Reverend Dudley Stokes, D.D., pastor of the First Parish Church of Carlton."

"Oh Angela," Tom laughed in relief, "did he ask you to sing solos in his church?"

"That," said Angela, "was his purpose in calling on me." She frowned suddenly. "How did you know?"

Tom wriggled with embarrassment and pleasure. "Anyone who had a church would want you to sing for them."

"I guess you're right," said Angela, "because the Reverend Mr. Stokes was very anxious to get me in his church before the other church snapped me up." She smoothed her apron and folded her hands over it. "I haven't made up my mind yet, but Mr. Stokes was a very pleasant young man. I wouldn't like to disappoint him." With her hands folded and a gracious smile on her lips, Angela gazed over Tom's head at the expectant congregation.

"Oh Angela," Tom spoke from the depths of his heart, "if only Daddy can keep the bulldozers from coming, we'll all be so happy."

"Amen," said Angela. She jerked out of her reverie. "I must help your mother finish up the parlor. I ought to be getting after that dirty old coat closet. I don't believe it's been cleaned for a hundred years, but your mother wants the parlor all finished before your daddy gets back, and she'll never get it done alone. You go upstairs like a good boy and play with the twins. They don't like being cooped up in the house, and they may be scared of the storm too, poor little things." She shoved Tom toward the stairs, and launching into "Fight the Good Fight" she made for the parlor.

Tom climbed to the twins' room vowing that if only Joe's place could be saved, he, Tom, would buy

173

Joe all the vegetables he could eat with his own money. He'd persuade Joe to come up and meet Angela too so she could see he was a sheep and not a goat. If Angela was sure he was a sheep, she'd bake cakes for him and see to it that nobody bothered him or drove him away.

AFTER LUNCH the thunder and lightning rolled away, but the rain continued hard and steady. Buddy emerged, somewhat shamefaced, from his corner in the kitchen and climbed upstairs to watch Tom while he made improvements on his snake cage. When the cage was finished, Tom set out on another search for the missing snake. As he crawled on hands and knees, and not very hopeful, into Elsie's room, the doll's house which he'd hardly noticed for weeks suddenly caught and held his eyes. In the gray afternoon light it positively sparkled under the electric bulb which Elsie had trained on it. Outside it was shiny gray with white trim and green shutters. Inside Tom could see the rooms all freshly decorated like the rooms in the big house. Elsie sprawled on her stomach in front of the doll's house. She was dabbing a paintbrush into the parlor and snatching back her hand before Paddy Paws, who lay full spread across the parlor floor, could snag it.

"Gee Elsie," exclaimed Tom, "you've sure made that old doll's house look beautiful." Still on hands and knees he crawled closer. The rooms, the halls, the closets, the stairways were all exact copies of the ones in the big house, and Elsie had almost finished with her decorating. Only the parlor, the dining room, and the downstairs hall remained to be done. "I bet it looks better now even than when Althea was a little girl," said Tom.

"I think so too." Elsie sat up and surveyed her work with satisfaction. "Only," she sighed, "there isn't any furniture. I wish I knew what happened to that furniture."

"Maybe I can give you some for Christmas," offered Tom. "I have to give you something."

"That's a good idea," said Elsie. "Of course it won't be the same, but it'll be better than nothing. When it's time I'll tell you exactly what I want." She turned back to her work.

"I'd just as soon help you paint," suggested Tom. "There's nothing else to do."

"Well," Elsie frowned, "I don't know that I can let you paint."

"I know how. I've painted a boat."

"This is different. I'll let you sandpaper the paneling in the hall, and maybe you can paint some later."

She handed Tom a square of sandpaper. "Get it all smooth. It'll take a long time. I'm trying to make this a really professional job."

Tom would rather have painted, but this was better than nothing on a rainy afternoon. Lying on his stomach he reached far into the hall and began to rub.

"Ow!" Elsie started back wringing her hand. "Oh, oh," she wailed, "I've spilled the paint."

From the parlor Paddy Paws emitted a nasty growl.

"That's the last straw." Elsie righted the paint can and scooped up Paddy Paws in her arms. "I don't care where you have your kittens. Go have them in the woods. I've been too good to you, and you're nothing but a mean, ungrateful old cat." She bore Paddy to the door, dumped her outside, and slammed the door shut.

"It's too much," she declared as she plumped down again to work. "That cat doesn't know the meaning of the word gratitude."

Tom went on rubbing. The old paint flaked off in white powder. He felt he was getting somewhere. He rounded the corner of the hall, and the door to the coat closet under the stairs pushed open. He wriggled his shoulders as far as he could into the hall and held the door ajar with one hand while he sanded with the other. A little black snake poked its head around the open door and slithered into the hall.

"Hey," Tom shouted. He grabbed the little snake and, extricating his head from the doll's house, he held it up in triumph. "Elsie, I've found my snake. It was in the coat closet."

"In the coat closet?" Elsie emerged from the parlor and stared at the snake as though she didn't believe it was real.

177

The snake wriggled vigorously in Tom's hand.

"It's lucky I found it," he said, "or it would have died trapped in there." He scowled. "I bet that little stinker Digby put it in just to be mean."

"No," Elsie shook her head, "I don't think so. He didn't know about the door, and anyway Paddy would have torn him to bits if he'd come that close, especially with a snake."

"Well, how did it get in?"

Elsie frowned. "I don't know. I've never opened the door. I've been working on other rooms. Let me feel inside the closet."

She squirmed into the hall and reached her hand inside the door. After a long time she backed out.

"Tom!" She grabbed his arm. "There's a little trap door in the back of the closet. It opens and shuts, and there's a little staircase leading down from it. I wonder why — "

"A staircase?" Tom interrupted, and pushing Elsie aside, he reached in to feel for himself. Sure enough, with his finger, he could open and shut the door and feel the tiny flight of stairs going down.

"There must be a hole somewhere around the bottom of the doll's house," he said as he emerged. "The snake must have crawled under the house and then up the stairs." He crawled to the back of the doll's house, and there, sure enough. in the skirting board, was a knothole just the right size for his snake. "I've found it," he announced. "Look, Elsie, here's where

the snake got in." He waited for Elsie. When she
didn't come, he crawled back to her. "I've found
where the snake got in."

Elsie nodded absently. "I just don't see why the
staircase is there. The cellar stairs go down from the
kitchen."

"Maybe the fugitive slaves just put it in for a surprise when they built the doll's house," said Tom.

"I bet they never thought a snake would use it."

"The fugitive slaves!" Elsie's back stiffened. "The fugitive slaves!" Rigid on her knees she stared at Tom.

'Well, why not?" Tom was getting up to take the snake to its cage.

"Oh Tom," Elsie's pigtails began to quiver, "do you suppose it's a secret staircase for the fugitive slaves?"

Tom laughed. "It's a secret staircase for snakes."

"You don't understand. The fugitive slaves used the secret staircase to get to the secret passage that goes between the river and the house."

"Oh Elsie, you're imagining things again. This is just a doll's house."

"Don't you see?" Elsie jumped to her feet. "The doll's house is exactly like the real house, exactly." She grabbed Tom's arm. "Oh Tom, do you suppose there's a real secret staircase in the coat closet in the hall?"

Tom's heart jumped. He almost dropped the snake.

"I thought there ought to be a secret passage or something when Miss Chapin told me about the fugitive slaves," Elsie went on in a rush. "Miss Chapin's grandmother didn't know about it, I guess. Maybe no one knew about it except Mr. Follonsbee and the slaves, and perhaps Althea. Do you suppose Al-

180

thea — " Elsie stopped with her mouth wide open and her eyes like saucers.

"Gee!" Tom felt his heart pounding. "Let's go see."

"Yes," Elsie caught her breath, "yes, let's. It'll be all right with two."

"I've got to put away the snake."

"Hurry up. I can't wait, but I'd rather there were two of us."

As they came down into the hall they could hear Angela and their mother discussing curtains in the parlor. Elsie pressed a finger to her lips and motioned Tom to wait while she slipped into the dining room. She returned in a minute with two candles and a box of matches. Tom followed her to the closet door. There she hesitated and shoved him ahead.

"It's the cobwebs," she whispered. "They make me scream. You go first and brush them down."

Flailing his arms Tom marched into the closet. Oddly, his fingers didn't feel any cobwebs. He beckoned Elsie in. They crouched on the floor and lit their candles. It was an ordinary coat closet with pegs around the walls. The plaster was stained and dusty. Some cobwebs hung in the corners, but the floor was quite clean, and this made it easier for Tom and Elsie to see the outline of the trap door.

"I told you," whispered Elsie. Forgetting to be afraid she dropped on her knees beside the trap door

181

and tugged at the iron ring which served as handle. The trap door swung up so easily and smoothly that Elsie almost fell head first down the flight of stairs. Her candle went out and she clapped her hand over her mouth to keep from screaming. Tom relit her candle. For a minute she stared down the black staircase, then she motioned Tom to go ahead.

"Cobwebs," she breathed in his ear. "I can't do it."

Tom gave her a reassuring pat and started down the stairs. By the light of his candle he could just make out the step directly below. Conscientiously he swung his free hand in front of him to remove any cobwebs. The stairs kept on down. There was no trace of a cobweb.

Just like her, he thought, always afraid of something that isn't there.

A second later Tom dropped straight down and landed hard on his seat. Stunned, shaken, and in utter blackness, he distinctly heard his mother's voice saying, "What was that thump?"

"Buddy scratching," replied Angela.

"I hoped it was Richard coming home," and after a pause, "I wish he'd come. It's raining harder than ever."

Tom moved his arms and legs to be sure he still had them. He did, and he still had hold of his candle as well. Shaking now for all the world like Elsie, he reached the matches from his pocket and struck a light. He was sitting on packed dirt. In front of him a passageway, walled and vaulted with brick, stretched dimly into blackness. Looking behind he understood what had happened. The last three steps of the staircase weren't there. Above him he caught a glimpse of Elsie's face peering down the stairs. In the candlelight she looked as ghastly as one of her own ghosts. Tom got up.

"Come on," he whispered up to her. "The stairs are broken, but it's all right."

Very cautiously Elsie descended and, assisted by Tom, slid without mishap from the last step to the ground. Holding up his candle, and remembering to keep careful watch on his footing, Tom led the way down the passage. It went straight for a time, dipped, and continued at a sharp downgrade.

"It's heading for the river," whispered Tom over his shoulder.

"I — I t-told you so," quavered Elsie. "It was for the f-fugitive s-slaves. P-please wipe away the c-cobwebs."

"There aren't any," said Tom, and forged ahead.

The packed dirt underfoot became increasingly moist as the passage went on downhill and, where it leveled off again, water dripped between the bricks overhead. Tom picked his way around puddles and through slippery mud. The passage seemed to be going right into the river. Tom squinted into the darkness beyond his candle flame. Far ahead he saw a point of light. As he went on, very slowly, for the footing was sloppier at each step, the light shone gradually brighter.

"We're almost there," he whispered back to Elsie. She nodded and gestured him on.

The light shone very bright now. Tom hurried forward, tripped, and fell flat, not on mud, but on boards. Splinters pierced his knees and the palms of his hands. Dimly, through the pain, he realized that the passage had widened into a sort of room, and that light was coming from a kerosene lantern. Someone was helping him to his feet.

"Tom," said a gentle, familiar voice, "you hadn't ought to have come down here."

"Joe," gasped Tom, "I — I — "

Elsie's scream rocked the room. Tom turned just as her knees buckled. She sank down on the threshold. Her candle dropped from her hand and went out. Tom ran to her.

"It's all right. This is my friend Joe. He's my best friend."

"Pleased to meet you," said Joe shyly.

Elsie shook her head. Her teeth chattered audibly. Tom tried to pull her to her feet.

"He's not a ghost," he explained. "He's real. Feel him."

He motioned Joe to come closer, but Elsie shrank so violently that Joe drew back and tripped over a pan that stood in the middle of the floor to catch drips.

184

"See," cried Tom. "He trips. He's real. He's my friend."

Joe nodded encouragingly at Elsie. "Poor little thing," he murmured. "I'm not a ghost, miss." He nodded and smiled. "Honest I'm not."

The sensation of being called "miss" had a stiffening effect on Elsie. She rose shakily. Joe hurried to pull out a box for her to sit on and at the same time stumbled over another of his drip pans. Elsie sank down on the box. Still dazed she stared at the underground room. It was round, walled with brick, but roofed with boards. A cot, the table with the lantern and a number of bags and boxes around the walls were the only furniture. Joe carefully put his drip pans back in place.

"Can't stop her leaking in a rain like this," he murmured apologetically.

"Where are we?" Elsie managed to speak.

"Right under the old summerhouse, miss," replied Joe.

Elsie looked up. "The old summerhouse," she murmured. Her eyes brightened. "Where they used to play dolls." She sat very still for a minute. "How did you find it?" She turned to Joe quite fearlessly now.

"I fell in," he replied.

"Through the roof?"

"That's right, miss." Joe nodded. "It was the first summer I come here. It looked like rain one night so

I come to the summerhouse to get what shelter I could, and crash I went right through the floor into here." He shook his head. "I don't know how many times I patched that roof, but come a real heavy rain, it still leaks." He got out his frying pan and set it under a new leak.

Elsie leaned toward him. "When you first fell in, did you find anything?"

Joe backed away and sat down on the edge of his cot. "Nothing as you need worry about, miss," he said after a long pause.

"What was it?" Elsie's eyes glinted. Her pigtails quivered. "Did it have anything to do with Althea? Oh dear, you don't know about her."

"Yes I do," said Joe. "Tom told me, but I wouldn't — "

"Did you find anything? Tell me!" Elsie strained and quivered like a hound on a fresh trail.

Joe shifted uneasily on the cot. "There's that old trunk over against the wall. If you was to look in that, you'd find some things as belonged to Althea. They're nice things. You look at them and don't trouble about anything else."

Elsie darted toward the trunk. Even cobwebs had lost their terror. As she lifted the lid and began to pore through the contents, Joe sighed and leaned back more comfortably on his cot. Tom, who had been standing all this time unnoticed, turned reproachful eyes on Joe.

186

"You might have told me about this hide-out."

"Why Tom, I just never got around to it. There was so many other things going on, and we was having such a good time, and, well, there was other reasons. You know, Tom, sometimes I wonder if maybe I ain't a ghost after all, only don't tell the young lady."

"Listen, Joe. She's not a young lady. She's just my sister, and you don't need to be so polite to her either. She's not used to it."

"I gotta be polite to her just because she's your sister. I'm real grateful to you, Tom. I can't tell you how grateful I am. I mean it."

"I haven't done anything."

"Yes, you have. You brought me the pie and cake. If you hadn't done that — " Joe shook his head and then jerked aside as a new drip landed on it.

"Aw, that wasn't anything."

"Why, without that pie and cake, especially the chocolate cake, I — " Joe stopped in confusion, rubbed his head, and started over again. "This afternoon I been laying here and eating that cake the boy dropped. I been eating it slow, and, Tom, I been remembering like I never remembered before."

"Gee, you better be careful," warned Tom, and he wiped a drip from his shoulder.

"That's right," replied Joe. "I feel awful queer, but it's a different kind of queer. It's not like when they're after me with the questions." Joe wiped

187

some more drips from his head. "I gotta do it," he said.

"Do what?" asked Tom. He wiped again at his shoulder, and looking up, he noticed that the drip had developed in a thin, steady stream.

"I gotta go up to your house and see," said Joe. "Would you mind taking me up to your house to-morrow and introducing me to Mrs. Gittens and your ma and pa too of course. I'd like to be introduced proper. Would you mind?" He looked eagerly at Tom while a steady stream of water trickled down his neck.

"I wouldn't mind. I'd like to." Vainly Tom tried to dodge between the drips. Water was trickling steadily from all the cracks in the roof. "Come on now," he urged Joe. "Come up the passage with us now. It's getting too wet down here."

"I don't know as I ought to do it so sudden." Joe shrank back. "I might startle them." Three streams of water poured over his head and shoulders. He shook himself. "I never seen it leak quite so bad as this." He looked at the roof and his face lengthened. He jumped onto his cot and pushed open a trap door in the roof. Water poured in. Joe stuck his head through the door. A moment later he ducked back and slammed the door after him. He stood still on the cot. Only his eyes moved back and forth over the room and its meager furnishings. Water dripped over his head and shoulders. His eyes finally fixed on

Tom and pierced his heart with their anguish.

"What's the matter?"

"The river," said Joe, "the river's coming right up over us."

Tom stared blankly. "A flood?"

"I guess so." Once more Joe's eyes swept the room. The water trickled steadily through the roof. "I guess it's finished." Joe's voice broke.

"Come up the passage with us, Joe," Tom begged. "We'll take care of you."

Joe stepped off the cot. "May as well," he muttered. "May as well do it now. There's nowhere else left." He stood with bent head and shoulders. "It was a nice little place," he said, "and it was mine." Suddenly his shoulders straightened. "No, Tom," he said with decision, "not now. I gotta see to my boat."

"We'll wait."

"No," Joe shook his head, "you gotta hurry. The water's rising awful fast. Light your candle. Miss, Miss Elsie, you gotta hurry back home." Elsie didn't hear him. Her head was deep in the trunk. He ran to her and laid a hand on her shoulder.

"Don't bother me," she said.

Joe shook her gently. She looked up. A trickle of water splashed on her nose.

"What is it?" she asked.

"You gotta go right back up the passage to the house. Don't get scared, but go quick. The river's flooded."

189

Elsie stared into Joe's anxious face. Aware, for the first time, of the water trickling over her, she shivered. "Flooded?" she asked. "How did it flood?"

"I can't be sure," said Joe, "but I suspect that old mill dam busted. It's rising fast. Hurry." He pulled Elsie to her feet and urged her toward the passage. Elsie balked.

"I've got to take the trunk."

"No," Joe shook his head, "you two can't carry it alone, and I ain't got time."

"But I've got to."

"You can't," said Tom.

Elsie's face collapsed tragically. "The furniture for the doll's house is in the trunk." Her voice trembled, and two streams of water coursed down her cheeks like tears.

Joe's look of anxiety deepened into one of consternation. He lifted his arms in a gesture of despair. "All right," he said, "I'll carry it for you, only don't cry."

He stepped to the cot, pulled a flashlight from under the blanket and handed it to Tom. He gave the lantern to Elsie.

"You go first." He walked her to the tunnel entrance. "I'm next with the trunk. Tom, you're the rear guard. Hold the flashlight steady."

Joe heaved the old trunk on his shoulder, and they set out slowly through water ankle high. As the tunnel turned up hill, the footing became more solid,

191

and Joe said sharply, "Now walk quick, and maybe I can get back in time to see to my boat and my other things."

Elsie stopped in her tracks. "I'm sorry. I didn't think. Oh dear."

"Don't fuss. Just walk along," ordered Joe, and the rear guard noted with approval an authoritative ring in the gentle voice of Joe. He sounded almost like Angela.

Joe lifted the trunk up the secret staircase and set it down carefully in the coat closet. From the parlor they could hear Mr. Stackpole's voice.

"I barely got over the bridge. I could see the water rising. Another minute and the car'd have been washed right off. A dam must have broken. It came like a tidal wave."

In the dimness of the closet Joe nodded sagely at Tom. "The mill dam," he whispered. He took back his flashlight and lantern and started down the staircase.

Tom seized his arm. "Don't go back. Stay here where it's safe."

Joe shook his head. "I gotta see to my boat. Don't want to lose that too."

The strains of "For Those in Peril on the Sea" rose and swelled through the house. Tom held Joe's arm. Joe paused while his lips curved in the expectant half smile. Gently he shook himself free.

"I can't just leave that boat," he whispered. "It's a

good boat. But I'll be back, Tom. You be watching for me at the kitchen door so's you can let me in and introduce me proper. I wouldn't want to come up out of the ground like this and startle them." He nodded at Tom and disappeared down the staircase.

Tom lit his candle, and by its flickering light he and Elsie looked at each other.

"I — I didn't think, Tom," Elsie whispered. "I wanted that furniture, but if your friend loses his boat or — or gets drowned, I'll smash it all to bits. Oh Tom, I hope nothing happens to him."

Tom saw tears, real ones, glistening on her cheeks. He patted her shoulder.

"Come on, let's find out what the lawyer told Daddy."

Having successfully beaten his way home through storm and flood, Mr. Stackpole was in much higher spirits than in the morning.

"Porter won't promise anything," he said, "but he thinks there's a chance that Creel's title to that land isn't clear. He's going to look into that first and he's got some other angles too. The more it rains, the better for us because Creel can't start work and Porter has more time. The main road was flooded in six different places, and if that bridge holds, it will be a miracle."

THE TWINS had spent a long, dreary afternoon indoors. They looked forward to the race with more than ordinary eagerness, and they were sorely disappointed.

"Let's feed them by the window," said Elsie, "so we can see him coming."

With Richard slung over his shoulder, and the cereal on the table just out of reach, Tom pressed his nose to the glass and stared into the dusk. Richard roared in protest as he reached vainly for the cereal and saw his brother getting off to a head start.

"He should be coming soon," muttered Tom. With his eyes still on the window, he absently picked up the cereal and began spooning it in the general direction of Richard's mouth.

Elsie laid down her spoon, and she too pressed her face to the glass. "I think I see water just at the bottom of the slope." Paul, seeing certain victory snatched right from his mouth, doubled up in a paroxysm of rage. Elsie dropped the cereal and made no attempt to pick it up. "Oh Tom, do you think he had time?" She got up and paced the floor while Paul roared and struggled on her shoulder. "Oh be quiet," she said, and disregarding all the rules she sat down, stuffed the bottle in Paul's mouth, and once more pressed her face to the window.

"I can see it too." Tom's voice caught. "It keeps coming higher." He deposited a spoonful of cereal in Richard's ear. At this final affront, Richard lost all self-control. His screams became hysterical. His face flushed from red to purple.

"Give him the bottle," shouted Elsie, "or Angela will be up."

Tom gave him the bottle and unmoved by his stricken, tear-laden eyes turned again to the window.

While the twins sucked and grunted in a contrapuntal chorus of discontent, Tom and Elsie peered into the gathering night. Glossy black water crept, inch by inch, beyond the woods and up the slope. The twins emptied the bottles and, whining in annoyance, squirmed and kicked in their trainers' arms. Still Tom and Elsie strained at the window, seeking some speck of light or moving shape on the darkening, swelling flood.

"He ought to be back," Tom almost sobbed, "he ought to."

"I can't stand it." Elsie stood up, lifted Richard from Tom's lap, and carried both twins to their beds.

Tom jumped up too, determined to run out and find Joe if — and his stomach went sick with fear —

if Joe could be found. He pressed his forehead to the window for one last agonizing look. A darker shadow seemed to be moving over the water. Tom strained his eyes until burning sparks and red balls swirled over the whole dim landscape and shadows emerged and faded like phantoms. Tom shut his eyes and held his breath. When he dared to look again, he thought — he was almost certain — that something like a rowboat was nosing through the trees toward the slope. It came out from the trees, shadowy still, but surely a boat, and a tall figure seemed to loom up in the stern. It must be Joe. For a minute Tom rested his head against the window, limp but ecstatic with relief.

"Elsie!" Tom came to life. "He's coming!" He dashed downstairs into the kitchen and flung open the door.

"Shut the door," said Angela. "It's raining."

"Someone's coming," said Tom. "A friend of mine's coming. He wants to meet you."

Angela turned from her cooking. "Thomas Stackpole are you crazy? Shut the door."

"I can't." Tom peered into the darkness. "He'll be here in a minute. He's been flooded out. He'll need some dry clothes and something to eat."

Angela came to the door. "If you'd talk sense," she said, "I might be able to understand you."

"Is he here yet?" Elsie bounced into the kitchen. "Oh Angela," she cried, "you'll like him. He's like a fugitive slave. He lives underground. At first I thought he was a ghost, but he isn't, and he risked his life to bring me the furniture for the doll's house." She jumped up and down at the back door.

Angela rolled her eyes to the ceiling. "Oh Lord," she cried, "grant me patience."

"Here he is," shouted Tom, then drew back with a cry as Digby Creel scooted in the door.

Digby was dripping wet and shivering, but his spirit was undaunted.

"Oh boy," he jumped up and down spattering muddy water in all directions, "you've missed all the fun. We've been flooded, and I helped Joe rescue us. I steered the boat. Oh boy, I bet you wish you'd been flooded."

Mrs. Creel, distraught and dripping, tottered in the door.

"I'm going to faint," she panted.

"You'd better not," growled her husband as he stamped in after her. "This house will go next, and don't think I'm going to carry you." Mr. Creel removed his hat and emptied several quarts of water from the brim onto the floor.

Angela placed her hands on her hips.

"Oh boy," Digby waved his arms and jumped harder than ever, "we're going to be flooded again. Oh boy!"

Tom darted out into the rain. "Joe," he called, "Joe."

Joe stood just beyond the light from the open door. Tom grabbed his hand.

"Come on, Joe." Joe hung back. "You're frozen. You're shivering." Tom pulled at his hand.

"I better not." Joe drew away. "I'm scared. I can't do it."

Elsie grabbed his other hand. "Come in this minute," she scolded, "before we all get wet. Do you want to make Angela mad?"

"N-no," stammered Joe.

With Tom and Elsie each pulling a hand, Joe shambled into the light from the open door.

"Here's the one we meant, Angela," called Elsie.

"Here's my friend," added Tom.

Angela stood at the door peering out. Suddenly her eyes seemed to glaze and bulge. Her mouth fell open. She raised one hand to her throat and then, like a great tree, she fell full length across the threshold. A minute later the electricity failed.

Without Joe and his flashlight, the Stackpoles could hardly have got through the next few hours. It was Joe who lifted Angela, carried her to the parlor couch, laid her there, and found a blanket to cover her. It was by the light of his flashlight that, after much rummaging, Mrs. Stackpole found where Angela kept the candles in the dining room. When these were lighted and carried into the parlor, Angela, who had lain till then perfectly still, moved her head and sighed. Mrs. Stackpole knelt beside her.

198

"Angela, are you better? What can I get for you?"

"I'm better," replied Angela. "Just let me lie still."

"Yes, you must rest. You've worked too hard. I shouldn't have let you work so hard in the heat."

"It must have gone to my head," murmured Angela, and she shut her eyes.

With help from Joe and his flashlight, Mr. Stackpole found some wood in the cellar and started a fire in the parlor fireplace. "We must keep her warm," he said, and Joe nodded in agreement.

Although Mr. and Mrs. Stackpole could not bring themselves to welcome the Creels very cordially, they could not ignore them either. Digby darted all over the place describing (though no one listened) how they had sat on the roof of their house calling, "Help, help!" while the water rose higher and higher until it was swishing right over their feet. Joe had heard their cries and come with his boat. "Oh boy," shrieked Digby, "oh boy!"

Tom was delegated to take him upstairs and get him into dry clothes. Tom performed this task with a very bad grace which Digby didn't even give him the satisfaction of noticing.

"Oh boy," chortled Digby, "I bet you wish you'd been there."

From the kitchen Mrs. Creel repeated shrilly that she was going to faint. When she tripped over Buddy, and he emitted a deep rumble of pain, she went all to pieces. Mr. Creel shouted at her not to be a fool. Didn't she know that she was going to have to get out any minute and make for higher ground?

She sobbed wildly, and Buddy, overcome by the sadness of it all, lifted his muzzle and bayed. Mrs. Creel was taken upstairs and put to bed in the spare room. Mr. Creel could not be so easily disposed of. At intervals he tramped out to measure the rise of the river and returned to announce with gloomy satisfaction that it was up four inches, or six inches, and they'd better get ready to evacuate. Digby hailed each announcement with shouts of joy and a general invitation to come on out and watch him swim.

Mrs. Stackpole and Elsie made efforts to prepare supper, but by the dim light of candles they couldn't find where Angela kept things in the kitchen. They had to keep running to the parlor to ask her. They stumbled over Buddy. They collided with the ubiquitous Digby. Their progress was painful and slow. Meanwhile Mr. Stackpole was trying to lend Joe some dry clothes. Joe resisted stoutly, declaring that he was warm as toast and dry as a bone. It was Tom who finally persuaded him to put on the clothes Mr. Stackpole had laid out for him. While Joe was changing in the bedroom, Tom, waiting in the hall, told his father all he knew about Joe, his place by the river, the secret passage and the underground room.

"His house and all his things are washed away, and if the bulldozers come, it'll be even worse for him,"

201

said Tom. "Please let him stay with us. He's the best friend I ever had, and when you know him you'll like him too. Elsie does already."

"I'm sure I shall like him," declared Mr. Stackpole. "As a man about to be dispossessed by Creel, I already have a fellow feeling for him. We must do everything we can to help him."

When Joe emerged from the bedroom dry, but extremely uncomfortable in the borrowed clothes, Mr. Stackpole seized his hand and wrung it.

"Tom's been telling me about you. I can't tell you how much I admire your independence and courage. I hope you'll stay with us as long as you want. I'm terribly sorry your camp has been flooded out, but I hope, I mean, Mr. Creel's house was pretty well covered with water too, wasn't it?"

Joe squirmed with embarrassment. "All over," he muttered.

"Ah," Mr. Stackpole rubbed his hands. "You were very brave to rescue them. I'll do everything I can to help you get settled again as soon as the water goes down. Can't afford to lose such a good neighbor and such a good friend to Tom." Again he wrung Joe's hand.

Joe tugged at his collar, which was too tight. He hung his head. "Oughta tell you," he swallowed. "I made them noises."

"What noises?"

"Them noises at night what frightened the young lady."

"What young lady?"

"Tom's sister, Miss Elsie, the one that believes in ghosts." Joe writhed inside the clean, tight shirt. "I shouldn't of come up after I knew someone was living here, but I heard the singing, and when I heard it, I was sort of drawn. Couldn't stay away." He rubbed at his neck and loosened his belt. "Never thought anyone would hear that old trap door squeak nor hear me jumpin' off the stairs. Never meant to scare no one. I just set there in the closet and listened to her sing. Just lately I oiled the trap and jumped more careful. Couldn't stay away though. Not when she was singing."

Mr. Stackpole took in this information slowly. "So it wasn't the pump, and it wasn't the furnace, and it wasn't a ghost." He patted Joe's shoulder. "I'm relieved. I had begun to believe it was a ghost myself."

"I ain't so sure I ain't," replied Joe solemnly.

"Ain't what?"

"A ghost," replied Joe. "I get this funny feeling, and," he turned to Tom, "you seen what happened when I come in."

"Oh Joe, you know you aren't a ghost."

"Well, Tom, I tell you I ain't so sure. I been remembering."

203

"Don't remember," cried Tom. He grabbed Joe's hand. "Come on, we'll go get something to eat and maybe you'll feel better."

Still shaking his head and muttering dubiously, Joe allowed himself to be led to the kitchen where Mrs. Stackpole and Elsie had managed, at last, to set out a simple and not very appetizing meal. Joe found it a heavy ordeal, sitting at the table and being waited on by the ladies, but he managed nonetheless to put away a good amount of food. Mr. Creel refused to eat. He stamped in and out and gave reports on the water level.

"It's rising slower," he growled, "but," he added hopefully, "it's still raining."

Digby emitted a final "Oh boy" and fell asleep with his head in his plate.

After eating, Joe went out to see to his boat. He came back with the news that the rain had stopped and the water was no longer rising. Mr. Creel grunted and carried Digby up to bed.

All this time Angela had lain perfectly still on the sofa. She refused every offer of food and drink.

"Just let me lie here," she said, "and watch the firelight. When I feel equal to it, I'll go upstairs."

"I'll sit up with her," said Mrs. Stackpole. "She mustn't be alone."

"No ma'm," Joe spoke with decision. "I'll sit with her. I can keep the fire going that she likes to watch, and I can keep an eye on the water to make sure it ain't rising no more, and I'm used to sleeping most anywhere so if I get sleepy I'll roll up with Buddy and be real comfortable. You all get to bed and no need to worry." Buddy ambled over to Joe, yawned, and leaned against his thigh.

It was late before everyone got upstairs. Left to himself, Joe went out to look at the weather. The sky was clearing and already the water had begun to recede. He returned to the house, got an armful of wood from the cellar, and bringing it into the parlor knelt to rebuild the fire. On the sofa Angela moved and sat up.

"Eddy," she said sternly.

"Yes, Ma," replied Joe.

"Eddy," her voice trembled, "I don't care if you're a ghost or not. Come here to me." She held her arms out to him.

Eddy came to her and timidly took her hand. "Maybe I am a ghost, Ma, but if you don't care, I don't neither." She drew him closer. "I didn't mean to scare you," he went on. "I done it all wrong, but I didn't know how else." He knelt by the sofa and for a minute buried his head in her lap. "I'm sorry I run away, Ma." He looked up into her face. "I done it so's I could come back a hero and you'd be proud of me for once." His eyes fell. "I ain't no hero, Ma. I'm just a tramp. Maybe I shouldn't of come back at all and scared you, but I heard the singing and I ate them pies and cakes, and I started remem-

2 0 5

bering again. Before that I didn't remember nothin'." Eddy's great shoulders heaved. He sobbed, and Angela laid her hand softly on his bent head. "I can go away again, Ma, but I don't want to."

Angela held him close. "The Lord sent you back, Eddy, in answer to my prayers. He was slow to act, but He did, in His own time, and He means that you should stay. Oh Eddy, I'm a strong-minded woman, and I don't shed tears, but I'm going to now because I'm so thankful."

Angela had a good cry, while Eddy leaned his head against her knee and, with tears streaming down his cheeks, smiled like a contented child at the firelight. When Angela had recovered sufficiently to ask questions, Joe or Eddy ("I still ain't quite sure which," he apologized) had trouble making everything clear.

"I never was no good at brainwork," he said, "and some of the remembering comes hard."

"Just tell me as best you can," replied Angela, "and I'll figure it out."

Slowly, fumbling, urged on by Angela, Eddy told his story.

He had volunteered to take an enemy machine gun up on a hillside. In the darkness he crawled over rocks close under the position. He threw his grenades. He rushed on the gun position. There was an explosion. Eddy remembered crawling, almost naked, and in pain, over rocks and through darkness, and then everything went black. He woke up in a strange house, among people who spoke a language he didn't understand. He didn't know how he had got there, or how long he stayed with them, but it must have been a long time because he got well and helped with the farm work. He never learned to understand what they said to him, but they spoke softly and smiled and gave him plenty to eat, and he liked staying there and working for them. They called him Joe. It was the one word they used that he knew, and he guessed it must be his name.

When one day they took him to a city and gave him to some army officers, and then smiled and shook his hand and left him, he was so sad he just sat down and cried. He could understand everything the army officers said. They told him he was an American soldier. They told him the war was over and they were going to send him back home, and if he'd just remember his name or at least what regiment he'd belonged to, everything would be fine. Eddy tried to remember, and the food was good, and everyone was kind to him, but it was noisy and crowded, especially on the boat, and the officers wouldn't leave him alone. They kept asking him questions. He wished he was back with those people he couldn't understand, or just alone by himself where it was quiet. After the boat came the hospital. They still kept right after him with the questions until he couldn't stand it and ran away. Eddy skipped quickly over the first months

207

after he'd run away. He'd been cold and hungry a lot of the time and scared all the time. Mostly he was scared they'd catch him and put him back in the hospital, but sometimes, when he was real hungry in a city he didn't know and no way to eat except somehow getting a job, he was scared they wouldn't catch him and he'd starve. He wandered over a big chunk of the country during that first year of freedom. For a while he hoped that in his wanderings he'd see a place he remembered, or maybe meet someone who knew him and could tell him who he was, but it never happened, and he gave up hope.

He found the river and the clearing by chance. He'd spent the winter in the South and worked north gradually through the spring and summer, and when the train slowed down going through Carlton he hopped off because he liked the look of the town. When, after wandering around the town and its outskirts, he came upon the clearing by the river, he knew right off that it was the place he wanted to stay. It was peaceful and quiet, and he didn't know it then, but it was like that song about cool Siloam that Angela used to sing to him. It made him feel contented and safe.

Angela nodded and stroked his head. "I know what you mean," she said.

The boat for fishing, a plentiful supply of fresh vegetables rotting on the vine if he hadn't picked them, and the underground house were all right there for the finding. It was as if the place had been made ready just for him. He still had to work winters, but he saved up his money to improve his place. In the winter evenings, he dreamed about it and to help out the dreams read books too about the birds and animals and fish that lived thereabouts. Thinking about his place and looking forward to vacations there he forgot to worry about who he was or whether he'd be caught. As Eddy told about his life by the river, his face shone with such happiness that Angela suddenly covered her own.

"You were happy then, Eddy," she almost sobbed, "happier than when I was bossing you around."

"I guess I was," replied Eddy, "but after I got friendly with Tom I had the feeling more and more that it couldn't last, and, well Ma, I was just a tramp."

"No you weren't either, Eddy Gittens." Angela lifted her chin. "You were a hero, and I've got a medal upstairs to prove it."

"Aw Ma."

"Yes I have, and there's a citation that goes with it."

"A what, Ma?"

"A citation. It tells how you were so brave that they gave you the medal even though you were dead, and it's signed by the President of the United States."

"He must a got me mixed up with someone else."

"Not he. He doesn't make mistakes." Angela's bosom heaved. "You see," she seized Eddy's shoulders

209

and gazed proudly into his eyes, "I was right. I always said you'd amount to something if you just did what you were told."

Eddy hung his head.

Angela caught her breath and turned up her eyes. "Oh Lord," she cried, "prevent me from getting bossy. Prevent me, Lord, prevent me."

CHAPTER 16

THE NEXT MORNING Tom was wakened by a shrill voice repeating, "Oh boy! I bet you wish you knew what I know."

"Go away," muttered Tom, and he buried his head under the pillow.

"Wait till you hear!" Digby took away the pillow. "Boy, will you be surprised!"

Tom reared up in a fury, then covered his eyes against the bright sunlight. Digby perched on the edge of his bed and bounced up and down.

"Joe isn't Joe. He's Eddy, and he's got a medal. Angela made pancakes. Eddy ate twenty-two pancakes, and I ate fifteen. I bet you can't eat fifteen pancakes."

"I bet I can," Tom jumped out of bed, "and don't tell me about Joe. He's my friend, not yours, and I know more about him than you do."

"You don't either. He's Eddy, and he's got a — " Digby dodged the shoe Tom threw at him. "You can't hit me because — " Digby stopped abruptly. He clutched his stomach. His eyes grew enormous.

211

"I'm going to throw up." He swallowed. "I really am." He dashed out the door.

It was late in the morning, and countless pancakes had been eaten before all the Stackpoles fully understood what Digby had known for hours. Joe was Eddy. When they had finished expressing their wonder, their happiness, and their fervent hope that Angela and Eddy would stay with them always, Eddy cleared his throat and, taking courage from a glance at his medal which lay on the kitchen table, stood up to make a speech. He thanked them all, especially Tom, for their kindness to him.

"Without Tom," he began, and went on at great length about Tom's virtues, while Tom blushed and Angela beamed proudly on them both. Eddy finished that part of his speech and hesitated.

"There's something you all oughta know about this house," he said. "It ain't nice, but, well, it happened a long time ago, and there's no need to feel bad about it now." He cleared his throat again. "That Althea what Tom told me about, her that come back here visitin' and left her coat and hat in the hall and never come to pick them up." He eyed his audience uncomfortably. "She had an accident. Now don't get scared." He fixed uneasy eyes on Elsie and drew a deep breath.

"Did she go down the secret staircase, Joe, I mean Eddy? Did she?" whispered Elsie.

Eddy nodded. "You're real quick," he said, "and

you know them three bottom stairs is broke. Althea fell, and she musta cracked her head hard because it killed her."

"Oh," breathed Elsie, "how do you know?"

Eddy drew another deep breath and held it until he looked as if he would explode. "I found the skellington, but don't get scared." He let out the breath in a rush. "It was laying in the passage just at the bottom of the stairs. I buried it nice and decent in the garden, and it all happened long ago." He sat down and wiped his forehead. "She hadn't ought've gone down them stairs," he muttered. "She'd got no business going down there."

Elsie broke the long silence which followed Joe's speech.

"I know why she went down there. She went to look at the things she'd left in the trunk. There are letters and gloves and fans and embroidery and some lovely party dresses, and at the very bottom there's the furniture for the doll's house. I think," Elsie went on softly, "that before Althea got married and went away she filled the trunk with things that she'd loved during her happy childhood. She hid it in the secret room so that when she came back rich and bought the house again, the things would still be there, and she could take them out and remember. Poor Althea," Elsie sighed.

"Gee, Elsie!" Tom exclaimed. "How do you know all this?"

"I've thought about Althea a lot while I've been working on her doll's house," said Elsie, "and feel that I sort of know her. I guess we're sympathetic, if you know what I mean."

"Miss Elsie," Joe's brow puckered, "I just got through tellin' you that Althea's been dead — "

"That doesn't make any difference," Elsie broke in. "We're still sympathetic, and I'm going to take care of her things just the way she wants me to."

"Miss Elsie."

"It's all right, Joe, I mean Eddy. You just don't understand, and don't call me Miss. Nobody does."

Stark reality in the form of the Creels recalled everyone from the tragedy of Althea. Very politely, for him, Mr. Creel asked if Eddy would row them across the river. From the other side they could walk to town and get in touch with relatives who would take them in. The river, like a large lake, surrounded the house on three sides. The bridge was certainly submerged, if not washed out.

"If there was any other way of going," muttered Mr. Creel, "I wouldn't ask you, but we can't impose on our . . . er . . . neighbors any longer."

Mr. Stackpole did not protest this statement. Leaving Eddy to make his own arrangements with the Creels, he strolled to the kitchen window and surveyed the proposed site for the twelve low-cost houses. A solid sheet of water, which came to within a few yards of the house, completely covered the stone wall and stretched on back into the distance. Mr. Stackpole stood a long time at the window staring in a puzzled way at a ruffled pattern which wound, snakelike, over the smooth surface of the water almost as if it marked the course of a channel. He turned from the window just in time to see that the Creels were leaving.

"Funny," he said, "that the river rose so much higher in that particular spot than in any other, and I wonder why it looks as if a current were running there."

Angela took a long look out the window. When she turned back, she steadied herself against the table.

"Excuse me, Mrs. Stackpole," she said, "but I must go to my room and rest. I am having delusions unbecoming to a humble Christian."

During the next week the river fell back gradually to its normal size. Its course, however, was changed. The clearing where Joe had cooked and lolled and called to the birds was now on the far side of the river, which flowed in a wide curve and cut through the middle of what was to have been Mr. Creel's housing development. It skirted Follonsbee's Folly on two sides and rejoined its old course a short distance below the summerhouse. Mr. Stackpole refused to worry about the dangers of erosion and future floods.

"That magnificent sweep of water sets off the

beauty of the house as nothing else could. I wish Amos Follonsbee were here to see it. We'll plant the banks with rhododendron and azalea." He smiled dreamily.

A moment later his smile faded, for the flood which had brought Eddy back from the dead, laid all the ghosts, and assured to Follonsbee's Folly a dignified, though somewhat expensive and precarious, old age had also brought tragedy. Paddy Paws was missing, and Elsie's heart was close to breaking. After being evicted from the doll's house, Paddy had apparently slipped outdoors and been swallowed up in the flood. Elsie searched every corner of the house, the stable, and the yard. There was no sign of Paddy. Elsie and Tom walked for miles through the country, at first calling, and then, as the days wore on, searching silently for what they dreaded to find. Buddy went with them, sniffing the ground in a confused way and whining at intervals to tell them that he was sorry he had such a poor nose.

Eddy, to his disgust for it was still his vacation, had been drafted for flood relief. He had to work all day, but as soon as he got home he rowed up and down the river searching and calling until dark. Sometimes he rested on his oars to listen to a bird song and whistle a reply. Sometimes he looked longingly at the fishlines lying in the bottom of the boat, but with a shake of his broad shoulders he always recalled himself to duty, and his deep voice calling "Come Kitty, here Kitty, Kitty, Kitty" reverberated over the water.

Elsie tried to drown her grief in hard work on the doll's house, but the print of a seven-toed paw in the parlor paint and a tuft of gray fur stuck to the bedroom wallpaper reduced her, at each attempt, to such floods of tears that she had to give up. Not even Althea's trunk and the doll's house furniture could take her mind from her loss. The trunk stood unopened in her bedroom with the furniture untouched in the bottom.

On the morning of the first day of school, Mrs. Stackpole went to the third floor to make sure that Tom dressed himself properly and to cheer and encourage Elsie.

"You look lovely, dear," she said, "and I know you'll get good marks in school and make lots of nice new friends."

"Yes," said Elsie listlessly, "I suppose so."

From the yard below suddenly rose the stentorian voice of Buddy. A minute later the speaking tube began to whistle. Mrs. Stackpole answered.

"Send down Elsie, quick!" Angela's voice boomed out. "Send her quick! There's someone to see her."

Elsie's dull eyes lighted. She rushed down the stairs with Tom and his mother close behind. Angela stood at the kitchen door pointing outside. Elsie raced to the threshold and stopped short with a cry. There on the doorstep, a little gaunt, but neat, poised, and proud as Lucifer, stood Paddy Paws. She was sur-

¹ounded by four fat kittens. At Elsie's cry Mr. Stackpole hurried to the kitchen. The twins crawled to the door and whooped with joy. Eddy ran in from the yard. Buddy barked and barked. The diamond panes of Follonsbee's Folly shimmered and glittered in the morning sun as Elsie threw herself down on the doorstep and embraced Paddy.

"Oh Paddy," she cried, "my darling Paddy, where have you been?"

Paddy broke into a purr and rubbed her cheek against Elsie's neck, but she never told where she had been.